P9-BZG-858

What Was She Doing, Coming Here? Answering His Summons Like One Of His Subjects?

Aliyah made up her mind to leave in a heartbeat, and spun around to face the guards who'd escorted her to Kamal's mansion. "On second thought, tell your boss…or prince…or king…or whatever he is that I won't see him, since I know what's good for me."

They gaped at her as if she'd grown another head and remained standing there like a barricade when she tried to go back through the door.

"Okay, if you know what's good for *you*, move out of my way." At her growl, they exchanged anxious glances then rushed away.

Suddenly that ominous sense of oppression expanded. It seemed to impale her between the shoulder blades just before a deep, rough-velvet caress of a voice did the same.

"It seems you've forgotten how things work. You can go only when I tell you to."

Dear Reader,

When the throne of a phenomenally prosperous desert kingdom is at stake, what will its heirs do to secure it? Anything, of course! In *The Desert King,* Kamal has to secure the throne by marrying the lover he'd scorned years ago—a woman who seems to despise him as much as he does her. But duty soon transforms into intense pleasure, and passion reawakens love and the need to resolve the heartache of the past....

The Desert King wraps up THRONE OF JUDAR, my first miniseries for the Silhouette Desire line, where I feel at home writing what I love best—irresistible heroes who meet their destinies in passionate heroines, experiencing tempestuous journeys of pleasure and heartache until they reach their gloriously satisfying happy ending.

Coming next is my royalty miniseries, The Castaldini Crown, set on the exotic Mediterranean island kingdom of Castaldini, where emotions escalate along with the stakes in the quest for the crown.

Look for it from Silhouette Desire in May, June and July of 2009!

I would love to hear from you, so please visit me at http://www.oliviagates.com.

Olivia

THE DESERT KING

OLIVIA GATES

Published by Silhouette Books
America's Publisher of Contemporary Romance

If you purchased this book without a cover you should be aware
that this book is stolen property. It was reported as "unsold and
destroyed" to the publisher, and neither the author nor the
publisher has received any payment for this "stripped book."

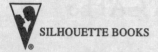

SILHOUETTE BOOKS

ISBN-13: 978-0-373-76896-7
ISBN-10:   0-373-76896-6

THE DESERT KING

Copyright © 2008 by Olivia Gates

All rights reserved. Except for use in any review, the reproduction
or utilization of this work in whole or in part in any form by any
electronic, mechanical or other means, now known or hereafter
invented, including xerography, photocopying and recording, or in
any information storage or retrieval system, is forbidden without
the written permission of the editorial office, Silhouette Books,
233 Broadway, New York, NY 10279 U.S.A.

This is a work of fiction. Names, characters, places and incidents are
either the product of the author's imagination or are used fictitiously, and
any resemblance to actual persons, living or dead, business establishments,
events or locales is entirely coincidental.

This edition published by arrangement with Harlequin Books S.A.

® and TM are trademarks of Harlequin Books S.A., used under license.
Trademarks indicated with ® are registered in the United States Patent
and Trademark Office, the Canadian Trade Marks Office and in other
countries.

Visit Silhouette Books at www.eHarlequin.com

Printed in U.S.A.

Books by Olivia Gates

Silhouette Desire

*The Desert Lord's Baby #1872
*The Desert Lord's Bride #1884
*The Desert King #1896

Silhouette Bombshell

†Strong Medicine #63
†Radical Cure #80

*Throne of Judar
†Stories featuring Dr. Calista St. James

OLIVIA GATES

has always pursued creative passions—painting, singing and many handcrafts. She still does, but only one of her passions grew gratifying enough, consuming enough, to become an ongoing career. Writing.

She is most fulfilled when she is creating worlds and conflicts for her characters, then exploring and untangling them bit by bit, sharing her protagonists' every heart-wrenching heartache and hope, their every heart-pounding doubt and trial, until she leads them to an indisputably earned and gloriously satisfying happy ending.

When she's not writing, she is a doctor, a wife to her own alpha male and a mother to one brilliant girl and one demanding angora cat. Visit Olivia at www.oliviagates.com.

At the end of my first-ever miniseries,
I again dedicate it all to the two ladies
who helped me bring it into existence.

My phenomenal editor Natashya Wilson
and Silhouette Desire's wonderful senior editor,
Melissa Jeglinski.

Thanks, ladies, for the incredible experience.

Prologue

Seven years ago

"Did you think I could just let you walk away, Kamal?"

Kamal froze. It was either that or stagger with the impact of that voice, that challenge. That presence.

Aliyah. Here. From the direction of her voice, on his bed.

So this was why his agitation had spiked the moment he'd stepped into his mansion. He'd felt her, even when logic had kept telling him it was the one place she couldn't ambush him.

But she'd done so already everywhere else. Why had he thought anywhere beyond her reach, her persistence? Her invasion?

He kept his unseeing eyes cast downward. It was only because they'd been focused there, crowded with inner visions of her, that he hadn't seen her in the flesh as soon as he'd entered his bedroom.

It was no use. He didn't have to see her for her to work her black magic. To turn him from the twenty-eight-year-old man who daily managed thousands of people, defeated moguls twice his age and assimilated their achievements on his ascent to global power into the idiot she'd enslaved the moment he'd laid eyes on her...

Ya Ullah, how *had* she gained entry here?

Did he need to wonder? She must have conned his men. Maybe even seduced them. What else could have made them risk his wrath?

More visions assailed him, images of Aliyah slithering over other men before she ran back to him, threw herself in his arms reiterating her longing and love, draining him of coherence with the force of her hunger. Her insatiable, indiscriminating hunger.

And she was here, gambling on the force of his own hunger, on his inevitable surrender to it, against all reason and pride.

"Don't you know I can't let you go? I *can't, ya habibi.*"

The endearment, *my love,* gasped in a hot, entreating tremolo, broke him. He gave in. Looked at her. He knew he shouldn't have.

She was spread on his bed, encased in lingerie designed to turn men into testosterone-driven dolts, her honeyed mahogany silk hair fanned around her thin shoulders, her endless legs arranged in a demure pose calculated to make him want to charge her, spread them, guide them high over his back and plunge into what they so maddeningly pretended to guard: the scorching center of her femininity.

This was how he'd dreamed of her, dreams that paled in comparison to reality. A reality she must have saved to use as an overpowering weapon during hardball bargaining, like now.

She'd never shared his bed or let him share hers. They'd met on neutral ground, made love—had *sex* on strange beds. She'd never arrived before him to prepare such a scene. And no matter how deep into the night they'd lost themselves in each other, or how spent they'd been afterward, she'd always left. And she'd always left first. She'd never slept in his arms.

Now her arms were stretched out, her hands trembling as if

with emotions too brutal for her thin frame to hide or withstand. Emotions he knew she didn't feel. Didn't have. Now her voice broke, as if she had nothing *but* emotions, raw and driving. "Stop tormenting me, *ya habibi*. Talk to me. Come to me. You know you want to."

Aih, he wanted nothing more. To silence all caution, to tear his clothes off, flesh rebelling against the crush of silk and cashmere, screaming to feel her beneath him, to thrust inside her, to expend his anguish in the tempest of her being, to wrench his pleasure from hers and be at peace.

But he'd never be at peace. The only woman he'd ever invited into *his* being, had allowed to extend her dominion over his mind, occupy his priorities and dreams, had been an illusion. He would have to learn to exist with the loss of her festering inside him, eating through him.

Just one last time.

The temptation, the weakness, hacked into him, like a saw slicing through soggy wood. She felt it, augmented it.

"You have to talk to me, Kamal, tell me what went wrong. You owe it to me, to us. I refuse to let you just walk away. I can't stop loving you. And I know you can't stop loving me, either. I *know* you haven't."

She knew him too well, and he hadn't known her at all. But he did now. He knew all about the perversions that polluted her mind and body and ran thick in her blood. The moment he'd gotten proof, he'd made his decision. He'd never succumb again, never seek exoneration for her. It was over.

Not that she'd let it be over. She'd pursued him, pretending bafflement and pain at his abrupt breakup, shameless in her efforts to get him to recant his decision to walk away from his six-month-long addiction to her.

And she'd succeeded in cornering him. Tonight of all nights. He wondered how she knew that his hunger had accumulated to such levels, he'd probably risk anything for one more taste of her.

Enough. He couldn't let her cheat on him anymore, couldn't even rant accusations at her. He couldn't bear to listen to the lies addicts like her were superlative at coming up with.

But her eyes—those seas of old-gold and sincerity—were roiling with the liquid silver of distress, beseeching his mercy, dictating his surrender. And against his roaring will, he obeyed, her beauty intensifying as distance evaporated, the scent of her arousal tugging at his guts, his loins.

Then, as his lips neared hers, preparing to sink into the trap of her surrender, he saw it. The relief. The triumph.

He jackknifed up, a geyser of rage and disgust—at himself—threatening to blow him apart.

Ya Ullah, he'd almost fallen for her again. He *still* wanted to let go and lose himself in the magnificence of her abandon.

But he'd be doing just that. Losing himself. He'd already lost enough of himself to her. And *b'Ellahi,* he was putting an end to the damage here and now.

"You want me to talk?" he snarled. "Tell you what went wrong? I tried to spare you, but since you've invaded my home and come begging for it in this pathetic way, I'll tell you."

Shock at his aggression rippled over her face, jolted through her, sent her scrambling up, gasping, "God, Kamal, don't—"

"No. You went to lengths I didn't think any female with the least brains or dignity would go to, to hear this. So hear it. I ended it because you sicken me."

She spilled off the bed, groped for her clothes. "Please, stop…"

He plowed on, scraping his throat raw. "You'll hear this to the end, the truth about yourself, what you thought you could get me too addicted to you to notice. The busiest whore in L.A. is more honest than women like you, sluts born in conservative cultures who drown in vices once they experience 'free' societies. You want to know why you are the bottom of the barrel? Because to you, vice is an indulgence, not a necessity."

She sobbed now. "Please…I—I'll go…just stop…s-stop…"

He grabbed her arm as she stumbled past him. "I thought you had the intelligence to understand what you were to me. A convenient lay while I had some idle hours during my time here. That's all."

She convulsed as if he'd shot her, tried to wrench away. He struggled with the urge to drag her to him, beg her forgiveness for the cruelties, his fingers tightening on her fragile arm, the tremors that racked her sending electricity arcing through him.

Then it all welled up inside him, like blood through a reopened wound. Every word, every sigh, every *lie,* every step as he'd watched her rush to another man's bed. One of many, he'd learned…

*Let her go…*now.

He somehow did, released her arm as if it were something fetid and slimy. "*Now* you can go."

She staggered away, and something splashed on his hand, seemed to eat through his flesh to the bone. Tears. *Her* tears.

The blast of agony, of fury, almost shattered his sanity.

She was at the door when he bellowed, *"Aliyah."*

She turned like a broken marionette yanked by a string. But through the performance of devastation, it was still there. Hope that he'd succumb at the last minute. Or at least leave the door ajar for another incursion. He went mad.

He stalked toward her, for the first time in his life not in control, not knowing what he'd do once he reached her. *She'd* done this to him. He'd loved her so much. He hated her more now.

He stopped with a restraint he'd thought she'd destroyed. Then he heard a rumble. Alien, crazy. His. "If you know what's good for you, you won't let me see you or hear from you again."

She seemed to crumble then, as if around the hope he'd pulverized. With a tearing sob, she stumbled out of his bedroom. Out of his life.

Where he had to make sure she'd stay.

One

Kamal ben Hareth ben Essam Ed-Deen Aal Masood's fist smashed into his inert opponent with a bone-crunching crack.

The bag swung away in a wide arc before hurtling right back at him like a battering ram.

Snarling, imagining it one of the people who had put him in this predicament, this *disaster*, he met it with a barrage that would have left anything living a mass of broken bones and mangled flesh.

A full thirty minutes into his rampage, his punching bag seemed to grin back at him, pristine and unimpressed with either his strength or his punishment. Leave it to something inanimate to point out the futility of his fury.

He caught it on its last rebound, leaned his face on its cool surface on a harsh exhalation of exertion and resignation.

It was no good. He was still mad as hell. Madder. The edge hadn't even dulled. Would the rage ever lessen? Would the shock?

The king of Judar was dead. Long live the king. *Him.*

Blood surged in his head again. His fingers dug into the bag.

The bag should have been his brothers. He'd bet they would have stood there and taken whatever he dished out.

And why not? After all, they'd gotten what they'd wanted. First Farooq, followed by Shehab, his in-total-control brothers had done the unthinkable—forsaken the world for love and dumped the succession to Judar's throne in his lap. Then, two days before he'd gone through the succession transfer ritual, the king's long-expected death had come to pass.

Now he would participate in a ceremony of a different kind. An ascension—or rather, as it was known in Judar, a *joloos*—a sitting down on the throne. Farooq and Shehab had become the crown prince and the spare, and they kept patting him on the back for taking the throne off their hands so they could live in a perpetual haze of domestic lust and breed princesses for Judar at light speed.

How he wanted to batter sense into them, to bellow that the women for whom they'd forsaken the throne would end up tearing out their hearts and treading on them. He *had* made his augury unadorned and brutal. He'd gotten identical answers from the brothers he'd once thought the most discerning men he knew. Serene glances and pitying voices telling him time would show him how wrong he was.

Malahees.

Muttering his verdict—that his brothers had had their minds licked away by the honeyed tongues of two sirens—he tore his soaked sweatshirt over his head, balled it up and slammed it against the wall on his way into the shower/sauna/dressing area.

If all Farooq and Shehab had done was set themselves up for destruction, he would have kept trying to save them. And as victims of witchcraft, they could have had his forgiveness if all they'd done was shove him onto the throne.

But now he had to marry the woman who came with it.

He still might have accepted this fate worse than life imprisonment had it been any other woman.

Any woman but Aliyah Morgan.

Ya Ullah, when would he lurch awake to find all this another nightmare featuring the woman he'd been struggling to forget for the past seven years?

But it wasn't a nightmare. It was far worse. It was real.

And in this nightmare of a reality, by a macabre twist of fate, Aliyah had become the woman the future king of Judar had to marry, to fulfill the terms of the peace settlement that would secure the throne and restore balance to the whole region.

He should refuse his brothers' abdication, insist one of them take back the throne. Then one of them would be forced to marry Aliyah, even though he had another wife…

He stopped in midstride, stared through the flawless Plexiglas wall into the marble and stainless-steel shower compartment, a fist balling in his gut, images deluging him.

Aliyah…marrying Farooq or Shehab, in either of their beds, writhing beneath them, driving them wild…

The fist tightened, wrenched, forcing a groan from his lips.

B'Ellahi, had he lost his reason again? How could he still feel the least possessive over a woman he'd never possessed in truth, who wasn't worth possessing?

He entered the shower, turned the heat up to rival his internal seething, hissed his pain-laden relief as needles of scalding water bombarded his flesh and steam billowed around him, engulfing him in its suffocating embrace.

Damn his power of flawless recall. It gave him an edge that made him rise in every field he'd decided to enter, to conquer. It was also a curse. He never forgot. Anything.

He had only to close his eyes to feel it all again. Every sensation and thought since the moment he'd laid eyes on *her.*

Until that moment, to him, women had been either beloved family, cherished friends, potential-mate material, or self-acknowledged huntresses who understood that he had no needs, only fancies to be roused with utmost effort and appeased, swiftly, irrevocably. He had yet to meet a woman who hadn't fallen into one of those categories.

Then he'd felt her gaze on him, and all his preconceptions had been blasted away. He'd approached her at once, and her cutting intelligence and crackling energy, her exhilarating openness about his equally powerful effect on her, had deepened her impact on him by the second.

Fearing his unprecedented involvement, his aides had cautioned him. Aliyah wasn't using her modeling profession to insinuate herself into the highest tiers of society, hunting for sponsors—she was doing far worse. Not only was she exploiting her unconventional beauty, but also her status as a princess of Zohayd, violating the rules of her culture and rank to catapult herself to stardom through scandal and controversy.

But Kamal, for once out of his controlled, focused mind with hunger, had rejected the cautioning. To him she'd been a miracle, something he'd thought he'd never find. A woman created for him. One who lived in the West but had her roots in his culture, an equal who "got" him and mirrored him on every level—the duality of his nature, the struggle between the magnate who abided no rules with the prince who knew nothing but. He'd thought it was fate.

And it had been. Fate at its cruelest, setting him up for the biggest fall of his life.

The ugliness of the discoveries, of that last confrontation, still lashed him. But only with anger at himself, for blinding himself that much, that long, for still being so weak he'd counted on others to make it impossible for her to reach him again.

Now it was others who'd given her access to him for life.

The accursed Carmen and Farah, who'd ensnared his brothers. His idiotic brothers, who'd succumbed to their wives' influence. The damned Aal Shalaans, who'd demanded this marriage on threat of civil war. And the miserable Aal Masoods, who'd considered the marriage a peaceful solution. But it was originally the king of Zohayd's fault.

King Atef was the one who'd fathered Aliyah then refused to acknowledge her. Then her American mother had given her up for adoption, and King Atef's own sister had adopted her... No, they were *all* to blame.

The mess of mistakes would have remained a secret if King Atef hadn't sought out his ex-lover and assumed the daughter she'd raised was his. But his ex-lover had adopted Farah only when remorse over giving up Aliyah had overwhelmed her. It had ended well for Farah. She was now the wife whom Shehab, the fool, worshipped.

But it hadn't ended well for *him*. It had come full circle, throwing him together with Aliyah, now permanently. Aliyah, the half-blood princess whom everyone in formal society pretended didn't exist, but whose debauched life in the States provided constant fodder for malicious gossip in the region's royal social circles.

It enraged him that an accident of birth could make kingdoms steeped in tradition and conservative values consider such a woman queen material and an instrument of peace.

To heap insults on injuries, she was pretending outrage herself. She'd more or less told her father, her *king,* to go to hell, that she'd rather die than marry Kamal.

He was certain she'd known the declaration would hurl its way to him, a challenge designed to goad him to rise to it.

And he would. He was damned if he didn't make her eat her words. But not for any personal reasons, he told himself.

This was for the throne of Judar.

He stepped out of the shower, every nerve stinging from the combined punishment of overexertion and physical and mental overheating. He tore a towel off the nearest rack and, without bothering to do more than tie it around his waist, he stalked out of his workout area and made his way to his offices.

The bodyguards who'd proliferated in number and intensified in vigilance since he'd risen to the rank of king-to-be faded into the background so as not to encroach on his privacy or purpose.

As if anything could. He'd lived with all kinds of infringement all his life, had learned early on to thoroughly tune them out. Right now, it would take an attacking army to distract him from his intentions.

He strode to his computer station in measured steps, came to a stop before the central screen, clicked the mouse, accessed his e-mail program. Two clicks brought up the e-mail address he'd acquired hours ago. He clicked open a new message.

He paused for a long moment, rivulets coursing down his chest and back from his still-soaked hair, his mind a blank.

What could he say to the woman he'd parted from on the worst terms a lifetime ago? The woman who would now become his enforced wife, his queen, the mother of his heirs?

Nothing, that was what. He'd *say* nothing to her. He'd give her an order. The first of many.

Inhaling a deep breath, his fingers flew over the keys. Two terse sentences flowed onto the screen.

He stared at them for minutes before his gaze gravitated to the name in the address bar. Aliyah…

How could it still wield such influence, strike such disturbance in a composure he'd thought unshakable?

It had to be echoes of the weakness he'd once had for her. Echoes of an illusion. As unreal as everything they'd ever shared.

He ground his teeth and hit Send.

* * *

The phone slipped from Aliyah's fingers, hit her lap.

She leaned forward, fighting down a fresh wave of nausea.

She'd almost forgotten how that malignant turmoil used to seize her, contort her emotions and reactions. She'd fought too long, too hard for control, and feeling it ebbing away again...

She should cling to one thing. This time, her upheaval wasn't being generated inside a chemically imbalanced mind. She had major-with-a-skyscraper-high-M reasons to thank for her current state. This was no overreaction brought on by drug residues, or worse, a resurrection of her old volatility, as had been implied.

Oh, no. This *wasn't* a pathological reaction. She'd bet every cent she'd ever made—and she'd made heaps—that no one would react differently if, after twenty-seven years of a turbulent enough existence on this planet they discovered that everything they'd thought they knew about their life was one convoluted lie.

And what a lie. It had been perpetuated by the very people who'd been the pillars of her existence, who'd now brought it all down around her ears.

Could she accept it all one day? That Randall Morgan wasn't her father but rather her adoptive one, that Bahiyah Aal Shalaan wasn't her mother but her paternal aunt, that King Atef wasn't her uncle but her biological father, and her biological mother was some American woman she'd never met in her life?

Yet everyone begrudged her her shock. They'd dropped the bomb on her and had expected her to gasp in surprise then shrug and carry on as if nothing had changed. They'd implied that her distress lasting for more than a couple of days indicated a return of her instability. They made her feel unreasonable for demanding time to grapple with the revelations, for resisting being shoved into this new persona and accepting her fate with a smile. That last call from her uncle/father/whoever-he-was had made her feel cruel for not rushing back to Zohayd to meet the woman who'd given her up for adoption, starting the chain reaction that had led to this point. This mess.

Well, she was *entitled* to her freak-out time. As she was entitled *not* to see said woman, or any of them. Not just yet.

And no, it wasn't only because they'd managed to twist the course of her life, past and future. She would eventually come to terms with the rewriting of her history and her identity. What she couldn't *bear* hearing or thinking about was the main disaster they were railroading her toward...

A sharp *ping* startled her. She set her teeth as she sat up. She had to change that irritating "new e-mail" alert. But to what? All available alerts were equally aggravating.

Sighing, she clicked the track pad and the laptop's screen woke up. Her e-mail program window swam into view.

It took three beats for her heart to stop.

Just when she thought it wouldn't restart, all the missed beats converged in a detonation that almost blasted the organ out of her ribs.

She choked as the name rippled across her vision, passed through the barrier of shock, sank into her brain, into the brand it had long seared there.

Kamal Aal Masood.

She collapsed back, lungs burning, stomach churning.

An e-mail. From him. The man she despised above all, the man who'd taken all the love and passion and dreams of her too-stupid-to-live twenty-year-old self and ripped them to shreds.

The man everyone was insane enough to say she had to marry.

Every muscle twitched with the enervation that followed the blow as her vision wavered over the screen again. There was nothing in the subject line. Just his name in the "from" area.

Figured. What could the subject line be, from the man who'd thrown her out of his life like so much garbage? To

Clinging Idiot? Re: Sickening Slut? Parting Threat Renewal Notice?

There was nothing to say. He'd said it all then.

So what had he sent her? More abuse? She'd welcome that now. It would be written proof of the ludicrousness of the political marriage everyone was talking about as fait accompli.

Her hand trembled over the track pad. The cursor shook across the screen, missed its target. Hissing, she squeezed her hand to steady it, returned it to the track pad, clicked the e-mail open.

She stared at the words for what could have been an hour.

We will have dinner to discuss the situation. You will be picked up at 7:00 p.m.

That was all. No closing. No signature.

We will have dinner. You will be picked up. Picked up...

Yeah, like he'd picked her up that night they'd first met.

She'd been so deluded she'd thought him the embodiment of the best of her dominant half's culture, a knight of the desert, with chivalry and nobility running in his blood. She'd thought him her counterpart, her soul mate, a man burdened with inherited status, struggling with its shackles, its distorting effect on people, overcoming its limitations while making no use of its privileges to become his own person and a phenomenal success. She'd done the same, even if her success had been nowhere as phenomenal.

She'd thought he'd seen through her hyper surface to the vulnerable soul inside, struggling to conquer her weaknesses, the one man who wanted more than friendship from her, who'd valued her as a person, didn't consider her as a means to access status and wealth or a pawn in royal games of pretense. She'd thought he'd never get enough of her. Then he had, had walked away without a word.

She'd gone up in flames of desperation, begging for an explanation, a reconciliation. He'd walked away time and again, as if she'd ceased to exist to him.

His dismissal had driven her over the edge. And she'd gotten what she deserved for disregarding all survival instincts. Kama had smeared her face in the ugly truth. What she'd thought a powerful love affair with her perfect match had been nothing but the sick game of a twisted hypocrite who'd exploited her and reviled her for falling for it.

And here he was, reinvading her life. Relegating her to being picked up like a pile of dirty laundry he didn't deem to touch himself.

That royal bastard. Literally royal. Regal even, in a matter of days, thanks to the weird game of musical chairs the heirs of Judar had played, leaving him the one poised to sit on the throne. Not that he needed a throne to be ruthless. He'd always swept through life like a scythe, cutting down anyone who didn't make way for his advance. And she'd been pathetic enough to consider his cruelty a strength, one she'd been desperate to be close to, to absorb a measure of.

And she was supposed to marry that bulldozer.

Or so decreed some archaic tribal stupidity. Thanks to everything her two sets of parents had done before she'd been born, she was suddenly the main piece in that political game, her only purpose to make one move. Marry the crown prince of Judar—its king in a few days' time—and produce heirs to the throne with Aal Shalaan blood in them.

To that she said, *like hell.*

And it seemed she'd get to say it to his face.

She looked in fascination at her hand. It was no longer trembling. And that was only the outward manifestation of the stillness that had spread inside her.

It was as if after two weeks of feeling like she was struggling to get free of an octopus, she'd figured out how to escape. Why keep beating away the octopus's tentacles when she could bash it on the head?

Especially when said head was six foot six of despicable male heartlessness and chauvinism.

She rose to steady feet and walked to her dressing room.

She started to undo her buttons, then met her own gaze in the mirror.

He'd invited her to discuss the "situation," as he'd put it. He hadn't even deemed her worth picking up the phone to deliver the invitation. Not that it was an invitation. It was an order. One he fully expected her to rush to obey.

No. She wouldn't bash the head.

She'd chop it off.

At the strike of seven, they'd arrived. Kamal's men.

Or rather, the men of his new status. The king's men. Dressed in black, deferential yet daunting. Two had come up to her condo and escorted her down to a three-stretch-limo cavalcade where half a dozen clones had been waiting. They'd turned every head on the busy street, some in alarm, the band of Middle Eastern not-so-secret service guys flitting around her as if she were their king himself, not just his summoned guest.

It had surprised her, this show of power. The bustle of pomp and ceremony. Kamal hadn't had an entourage in the past, had rejected the fuss, the servitude, the imposition. Being royalty herself, she'd known that, as a prince of one of the most powerful oil states in the world, he'd had bodyguards following him. But she'd never felt them, let alone seen them. It had been another thing that she'd loved about him. Fool that she'd been.

Beyond lack of an entourage, he'd also never flaunted his inherited status or acquired power. Yet even people who didn't know him had always responded to his innate authority and had launched themselves at his feet. She'd been a victim of that influence herself. And he'd found their—and her—fawning abhorrent. He'd told her so.

Seemed he'd changed his mind.

That must be just one of many things that had changed about him. All for the worse, no doubt. If there could be worse than what he'd been. Whatever worse was, she was sure he'd managed it.

God help Judar and its entire surrounding region.

As for her, she'd help herself, just as she'd learned to do, thank you very much.

She inhaled on renewed purpose and stared at Los Angeles rushing by through the smoky, bulletproof window. She recognized their route. She'd taken it many times before. To his mansion by the ocean.

He'd always world-hopped, he'd told her, never staying in one place outside his kingdom long, never bothering with more than rented, serviced lodgings. Then he'd bought that mansion a week after they'd met. He'd given her the impression that he'd bought it for her. He'd implied he'd leave only when necessary, would always come back. He'd given her every indication that he'd been thinking long-term.

Now she guessed that a thirty-million-dollar mansion had been the equivalent of a thirty-thousand-dollar car to her. Too affordable to indicate commitment. And to a playboy of his caliber, six months must have been his definition of eternity.

Even though that mansion had been a beacon of hope to her, she'd never risked staying there overnight. She'd never stayed the night with him at all. She'd been terrified that during the intimacy of nights under the same roof, he'd see more manifestations of the imbalance she'd been battling, that he might have despised her for it.

She shouldn't have worried. He'd despised her anyway.

Suddenly it was there, at the end of the palm-lined road that sloped up the hillside to overlook the breathtaking panorama of the Pacific. The mansion that had dominated her stupid dreams just as it did the parklike gardens it nestled amongst.

She'd been there only in passing but knew that it boasted over thirty thousand feet of living space—not counting the porches, terraces and interior patios—and spread over two hectares. He'd told her it was perfect for all purposes—entertaining, accommodating guests, nurturing a large family.

She'd weaved a whole tangled web of fantasies around those last words, which he'd tossed in without meaning a thing. She'd thought this mansion the most beautiful place she'd ever seen.

It wasn't really. Being born of the royal family of Zohayd, she'd seen and lived in some mind-boggling places. Nothing in the States had ever come close to their sheer opulence and artistic extravagance. But this modern, pragmatic mansion had sheltered Kamal and her dreams of a future with him there, and so had surpassed perfection in her eyes. No wonder he'd thought her sickeningly pathetic.

The cavalcade stopped in the driveway. She exhaled a breath she hadn't known she'd been holding, rolled her shoulders as if in preparation for a wrestling match and stepped out of the car.

The two men who'd escorted her from her condo rushed ahead of her up the dozen stone steps leading to the columned patio. Two others followed, while two more materialized out of nowhere to open the main oak double door for her.

The moment she stepped inside, she felt enveloped by a presence. His. Could it be she remembered it still?

Seemed she did. She felt it in the austerity and grimness of the open spaces, the minimalist furnishings, the neutral color scheme and ingenious, indirect lighting. Strange. The decor had been exactly the same before, but then it had felt warm, welcoming.

Those impressions must have been all in her lust-hazed mind. Now she was seeing the place for what it was—a sterile space infected by the black soul of its owner.

They approached a ten-foot-high paneled double door. She

didn't know what kind of room lay beyond it. Probably some waiting room for her to stew in while their lord was fashionably late.

She reached out to the handle and both men almost fell over her to open it for her.

She sighed. She'd lived in the States the last ten years, had almost forgotten how it felt to be part of a royal family, guarded and served and smothered 24/7. Not that she thought this rising sense of oppression had anything to do with them. It had to be all about laying eyes again on the man she'd once worshipped and who'd almost destroyed her… She stopped just before she crossed the threshold.

What the *hell* was she doing, coming here? Answering said man's summons like one of his almost-subjects?

She made up her mind within a heartbeat, spun around. "On second thought, tell your boss…or prince…or king…or whatever he is to you, that I won't see him, since I *do* know what's good for me. Thanks for the ride. It was nice. I'll find my way back home."

They gaped at her as if she'd grown another head, remained standing there like a barricade when she started back toward the main door.

"Okay, if you know what's good for *you,* move out of my way."

At her growl they exchanged anxious glances then rushed away, disappearing outside the mansion in the space of two blinks.

Whoa. What was that all about? She wasn't that scary.

Suddenly that sense of oppression seemed to expand, and the influence that she now realized had sent those men running sharpened. It impaled her between the shoulder blades, just before a deep, deep drawl did the same.

"It seems you've forgotten how things work. You can go only when I tell you to."

Two

Aliyah froze.

That voice. The rough-velvet caress, the hypnotic spell that had once sent her spiraling into a realm of extremes.

It was coming from behind her. From the room she'd decided not to enter. Tranquil, indolent. A laser drilling into her from back to front, passing dead-center through her heart.

Somehow, her heart kept beating. More like rattling like a half-empty piggy bank in her chest. Her nerves kept discharging. Not that having a heartbeat and nervous transmission meant she could move. She couldn't.

The split second she could, she'd continue on her way out, show that overbearing lout how things worked. Surely not his way.

The spike of outrage thawed the grip of paralysis, freeing her legs, fueling three long strides on her charted path out of his trap. On the fourth she faltered.

What was she doing, walking away? She was here to see about one overripe head. She should go harvest it.

She turned around, walked back. The hardwood floor beneath her feet felt like soggy sand, and her legs felt powered by someone else's will.

As long as it wasn't his, she was fine with it.

She crossed the threshold this time, scanned the dimly lit room. For the first dozen heartbeats, she saw nothing.

Then he seemed to materialize out of nowhere, registering on her retinas, facing her in a high-backed black leather armchair at the far end of the room, framed by French windows that opened to the terrace leading down to the gardens. His body was relaxed, silhouetted in the golden light of a side lamp. His face was in darkness.

Her heart jangled into a higher gear. He was so still, looked so…sinister crouching there like a supernatural creature, half here, half in another realm, his face, his intentions obscured…

What a load of spectacular stupidity. There was nothing supernatural about Kamal. Except his supernatural ability to piss her off, playing all mysterious and lordly and…bored.

She moved, one foot in front of the other, each one a triumph of steadiness, advancing into the field of light cast by another tall lamp, her eyes fixed where his eyes should be, trying to discern whether he was looking at her, or if, as in the past, he was pretending she didn't exist.

One thing she did know—he was baiting her.

Expecting her to lose her cool? Or her nerve, as she had done so dependably in the past? Well, he was in for a surprise.

Meet the new Aliyah Morgan, buster. Or as it had turned out, Aliyah Aal Shalaan.

He was moving now, sitting forward as if her every step nearer was tugging at him, light creeping across his face like the sun at dawn.

She almost squeezed her eyes shut, dreading the moment his eyes would be illuminated. Then they were, striking a flare that knocked the breath from her lungs as he'd once knocked sanity from her mind.

It was his expression that jogged sanity back into place now.

Stunned? How could he be, when he'd been ready for her? When he had no human components to stun?

Now he was getting up, slowly, eyes narrowing to slits below the intimidating brows, a dark, towering force inundating her with emanations she felt would knock her off her feet if she didn't watch it.

Had he always been this way? Or had she forgotten?

With her photographic memory, was that even a question? While it had helped her forge a career for herself as an artist, the inability to forget had always been her curse.

She'd forgotten nothing. Not an inch, not a hair. He *had* changed. And infuriatingly, not for the worse as she'd been hoping on the way here. The twenty-eight-year-old sleek panther of a man who'd ruled her emotions for six months then abandoned her to the most chaotic, traumatic time of her life had been upgraded. And how.

But one thing was the same. His clothes. He was dressed the same way he had been the night she'd first laid eyes on him.

Had he done that on purpose? Could he even remember what he'd worn then? He'd once told her that he, too, forgot nothing.

But if he had remembered, had done it on purpose, *why?* To mock her? To goad her? To rewind to the beginning and start over?

Heh. Sure. As if.

He could start over in hell, where he belonged.

Still, it was the sameness of the sans-tie, formal charcoal suit with its unbuttoned silk shirt that echoed the color of his whiskey eyes that made the change so obvious, that detailed how the leanly muscled, broad-shouldered six-foot-six frame she regretfully remembered in distressing detail had bulked up with premium maturity to reach a new zenith of virility.

Problem was, the upgrade didn't stop there. The same magic had taken a chisel to his incredible face, turning his singular features from arresting to overwhelming. Worse still, the jet-black satin that was his hair and that he'd always cropped close to his awesome head now lay in luxurious layers down to his collar.

Worst of all was the addition of a trimmed beard and mustache. Those betrayed his true nature, showed him for what he really was. One of nature's most menacing entities. Not to mention one of its grossest examples of injustice.

No two ways about it. The years had been criminally kind to him. Seemed infinite wealth and power agreed with him. He'd no doubt improve exponentially the longer he had them, the older he got. And judging by his notorious reputation as a womanizer—the double-standard pig had dared call *her* depraved—every female with a brainwave agreed. And wanted a part of him.

And they could have him, could pick his bones clean, preferably. He no longer affected her… *Liar.*

Fine. So she'd be dead and buried before a male of this caliber didn't access her hormonal controls. What did it matter that he was the most magnificent male to walk the earth, a species of one? It changed nothing. Out of the few billion men alive, he was the one who she knew from mutilating personal experience was a soulless bastard. She wouldn't come near him with a ten-foot pole. Unless it was to poke out his eyes with it.

But none of that mattered now. Now she hoped only that she hadn't gawked at him too long. Not with her mouth hanging open, at least. What mattered now was that she regained the composure he always seemed to rob her of just by training those eyes on her. For once she needed to stand with him on equal ground.

She inhaled, cocked her head, forced her gaze to sweep him, down then back up to his eyes, smearing him with disdain.

"These sure are desperate times we live in."

For a moment she was stunned to hear her own voice.

So it was a husky wisp of sound, but at least she got it to work. Encouraged, enraged further by the way he remained staring at her as if at an unsavory species, she elaborated.

"They have to be, if your countrymen are scraping the bottom of the barrel to find themselves a king."

Kamal almost lurched. At the satin lash of the voice he'd just discovered had never stopped echoing in his mind. At the slap her condescension had landed on his stunned senses.

He would have if he could.

He couldn't even blink, couldn't access one voluntary action or thought. And the loss of control only spiked his outrage.

Was he doomed to react this way whenever he laid eyes on her? What was it about this woman that deactivated his rational centers? And activated his incoherent ones?

And she wasn't even the same woman. She'd changed, almost beyond recognition. Contrary to his every projection. And, *e'lal jaheem*…to hell with it, for the best.

His senses soaked in the changes, making feverish comparisons with her past self.

Gone were the wild clothes, the reed-thinness and crackling energy. In their place was a superbly dressed woman with a measured grace, a steady gaze and a body that had filled with a femininity so distressing it had everything male in him overriding all. His mind might be averse, but his body roared for its mate….

She isn't your *mate,* ya moghaffal. *She's anybody's.*

But his body was oblivious, was fighting all connections with his mind, bucking off its reins, struggling to break its control and claim the body that had stopped him from finding anything beyond frustration with others.

It was merciful that she contributed her own deterrent as she now made a dismissive, derisive gesture in his direction.

"That they've stooped to settling on you is the loudest possible statement that this world is going to hell in a handbasket. Judarians must be mourning not only their king's death, but their once-great nation's future."

There they came again. The insults. White-hot pokers designed to prod him into an uncalculated response.

He bit into the surge of tingling in his lower lip, into the urge to retaliate, to override.

So, that had changed, too. Her methods. Her approach. There'd clearly be no more breathless adulation spilling from those deep rose lips. Instead she seemed bent on bombarding him with condescension and contempt. And she was letting him know right off the bat, in lieu of the greeting they didn't owe each other. She had even before she'd laid eyes on him, coming all the way here only to turn around and hurl his parting words back at him, and through his men, too, just to make sure the slap landed effectively.

He'd bet she'd calculated, even counted on that to ratchet up his interest. That had remained the same, then. The masterful manipulation. In the past, her machinations had worn the guise of erratic spontaneity and had wrung the same response from him. She'd just changed her strategy to suit their tarnished status quo and the new poised creature she was now projecting.

And *b'Ellahi*—it was working. Spectacularly. When it shouldn't. When he shouldn't let it.

He could do nothing else. She'd walked in here training those fathomless eyes on him, her gaze familiar yet someone else's, throwing his own choice of cruelty back in his face and taking the wind out of his sails. Worse, she'd knocked him off course.

He'd intended to railroad her, unilaterally charting the rest of their regretfully unavoidable union. He'd summoned her here to inform her of his plans, and her role in them: to abide by them.

But she'd thrown down the gauntlet. And he could no more not pick it up than he could stop breathing.

It was beyond him not to engage her.

Shaking off the last of his paralysis, realizing he was about to hand her a measure of control, he twisted his lips, let his gaze run in enraged delight down her new ripeness.

"I agree. It did take desperate times to make me recant my decree of never laying eyes on you again."

Those strong, supple shoulders jerked with an incredulous huff, bringing thick, undulating locks of the gleaming mahogany that had grown to a waist-length waterfall splashing over breasts snug and full in her cream jacket. "Recant your *decree?* Better watch it. You're a breath away from having a hyperpretentious crisis and falling into a pompous coma."

He wouldn't. He couldn't.

But it was no good resisting. Amusement surged to his lips, tugging them into a painfully grudging smile. But it didn't stop there, burst forth in a guffaw.

Ya Ullah, she was yanking at his humor, as well as his hormones. The witch was still the only one who knew what to say and how to say it to appeal to his demanding sense of the absurd.

The one thing that cooled the heat of his chagrin at his helpless response was its effect on her. Her gaze wavered, her body language losing its confrontational edge. A laugh had been the last thing she'd expected, too. So what *had* she expected?

In answer to his unvoiced question, confusion flooded her eyes, her stance, spreading something too akin to mortification in his chest. And he knew what she'd expected. What she'd been trying to initiate. A fight. Dirty and damaging.

She'd expected him to tear back into her, more vicious than she'd been, to give her carte blanche to go all-out in turn. She'd expected this to spiral into another confrontation echoing the savagery with which he'd severed their liaison. But she'd intended to be an equal opponent this time, had drawn first blood, had intended to leave the battleground bloody yet victorious.

He should oblige her. Should let her show him what she had. Then he would show her, once and for all, who had the upper hand, that this was no democracy, that he'd settle for nothing less than total and blind obedience and that he *would* get it. He should let her know she had no say, no choice, could only save herself the indignity of being cowed by giving in first.

What he should do, and what he wanted to, were poles apart.

Without volition, he found himself moving toward her, in what thankfully must look like measured, tranquil steps when in reality they were impeded by the upheaval she'd kicked up inside him.

Her eyes widened as he approached her, and he almost groaned as her every detail came into sharper focus, the incredible mix of her Middle Eastern and Caucasian genes conspiring to form a beauty like no other.

The heart-shaped oval of her face still boasted that masterpiece bone structure, if it looked far less chiseled now that flesh softened contours that had been more skin over bone in the past. Her nose seemed less sharp, its slightly turned-up end even more overpoweringly elegant. Her lips, which had once spread so easily in eager smiles, looked even fuller, more ripe. But it was her eyes, as always, that struck him most and held his focus. Those mesmerizing eyes of hers, fringed by an abundance of black silk, their shape unique, their color even more so, chocolate fueled by the sun. Brand names had paid fortunes to have those eyes look out at the camera in dozens of high-profile ads. But they were far more hard-hitting now that they'd lost that intense, hungry look they'd been famous for.

He wouldn't even look below her neck. His general look from afar had caused enough damage.

He found himself two steps away from her, looking down the inches between them. In two-inch heels, she stood a glorious six feet high. A rush of pleasure filled him at not having to stoop to look into someone's eyes, into a woman's.

Aih, *lie to yourself. You've only missed this*—her *height*, her *presence*, her *eyes looking back at you*. Her.

It was better to acknowledge his weakness, to deal with it, rather than fight it and lose more to its dominion. This encounter wasn't going as he'd intended, so he'd better go with it wherever it intended to go and improvise along the way.

He cocked his head at her. "Got whatever baggage you have against me off your chest? Or do you need a few more minutes of uninterrupted abuse?"

She raised her eyebrows, now dark, dense wings when once they'd been plucked to about one third of their true exquisite shape. "Baggage? Try a load of justified antipathy. And statement of fact can't be categorized as abuse."

His lips twitched again. "Watch it. You're on that slippery slope to pompous coma yourself."

Her lips twitched in answer, twisting his guts with the need to crush them beneath his. "I'm not the one who slipped and fell on a throne and had its fumes of grandeur go to his head."

His smile widened, fatalism setting in this time. There was no point resisting the inevitable. "I assume the grandeur dig is about sending royal guards to fetch you?"

"Actually it started a bit earlier than that. With a subject-less e-mail graced with another of those decrees of yours. You're one of a few living men who can literally be called a royal pain."

He huffed a chuckle. His brothers shared that opinion, but even they hadn't put it so succinctly. "You're a royal, too—and a pain among other things—even if you choose to disregard the fact. So you still object to the royal treatment?"

Her gaze ran over him again, sweeping aside another portion of his restraint. "Once upon a time I thought you did, too. But I was a space cadet back then. I would have believed anything. I've long since landed on terra firma."

He stared at her. Into her eyes. And realized what was so different about them. Their pupils. Those used to expand and constrict almost constantly, turning their every glance into a live wire that electrocuted him whenever they fell on him. He'd realized too late that had been a sign of her chemical dependencies. Those pupils were unwavering now.

Other signs of her addiction—the malnourished tinge to her complexion, the fragility of her flesh and bones, the fluctuating energy that used to emanate from her—were also gone. She was now the picture of health. And stability.

He'd first attributed the changes in her to the weight gain that had followed quitting her modeling career. But now...could it be? Had she somehow overcome her addiction?

If she had, it was a miracle. And he'd believed there were no miracles in addiction. But even if she was in rehab, she must have been clean for years. This level of stability and health wasn't reached in less than that. He knew, only too well.

So had she been trying to beat her addiction all along? And with the clear evidence that she'd succeeded, shouldn't he have stuck by her, as he'd intended to do before he'd found out about the rest of her vices?

B'Ellahi, he'd just answered himself, stating the irrefutable reason he'd owed no support to the faithless wretch she'd been.

No. He couldn't have acted differently in the past.

But this was the present where it was no longer personal, where everything had changed, starting with her. Fate had decreed she was no longer a disgrace but the solution to a huge mess. And she seemed to have realized how damaging her earlier excesses had been. Now she should understand the need to heed the expectations that came with her new status.

Not that she did. Seemed this new stability didn't extend to responsible behavior.

He pursed his lips on the too-welcome surge of animosity. "It doesn't seem you've landed anywhere firm. I am told you're still as erratic and as irrational as you ever were."

She gave him a bored look. "You are told? By little royal tweeties, no doubt. Erratic and irrational, huh? According to whose rulebook of stability and rationality?"

"According to the one universally accepted by our species."

"That'll be the day, when the whole species agrees on anything, let alone the rules of rationality."

"Maybe that *was* too generalized. It was doomed to be false."

Before she could revel in his concession, he moved, clamped a hand on her elbow. She jerked in surprise. And response. He knew it. That same response was jolting through him, lodging in an erection that was developing the consistency of rock. And all he'd done was touch her through her jacket and blouse. But then, he'd been semihard just thinking of her, had been fully aroused since he'd heard her voice. He could only liken his condition now to a seizure.

Why wasn't life simpler? Why did he have to heed logic and pride and duty? Why couldn't he just drag her to the floor and feast on her, with no past, present or future considerations?

Before he was tempted to do just that, he gave her a tug in the direction of the terrace before releasing her elbow as if it burned him. "Hurl whatever insults you like at me over dinner. In my e-mail, I did promise a meal."

She darted a step away, taking her eyes into shadow. He couldn't read her reaction. Then her lips twisted. "You sure? Food will only give me more energy and make the invectives come easier."

Shaking his head at the exhilaration her every word caused to rev inside his chest, his lips widened again. "They *can* come easier? This I have to hear." Then, tamping down on the clamoring urge to snatch her into his arms, he gestured for her to precede him.

With a last considering tilt of her head, she turned and headed to the terrace. He walked behind her, devouring her every nuance and move, hormones a scalding stream in his arteries.

They stepped out onto the terrace where the waxing moon had just turned gibbous, illuminating the sky, dimming the stars and casting rippling silver over the infinity of the ocean.

She took in the view, her arms hugging her midriff. Her scent, free of artificiality, unchanged, unforgotten, the very distillation of sensuality, rode the gusts of gentle summer breeze, enveloping him. He ground his teeth on another surge of lust, bypassed her, walked to the table laid out with the meal kept hot over gentle flames. His hands tingled over the back of a chair, then with an inaudible curse, he pulled it back for her.

She arched one eyebrow at his gesture, then pointedly walked to the other chair and sat herself down.

Aiw'Ullah, that was what he deserved for succumbing to his moronic, chivalrous programming around her.

He sat down in the chair he'd pulled back, realized it had been a good thing she'd refused to sit in it. He had the lights coming from the room at his back. This way he'd remain in relative shadow as he wallowed in the infuriating pleasure of poring over her beauty, which was bathed in both artificial and natural light.

He watched her as she sampled what he'd ordered of appetizers, food unique to Judar. Her evident appetite and enjoyment boosted his viewing pleasure. Here was another thing about her that had changed diametrically. She used to be almost anorexic, a state he'd later realized had been induced by the drugs she'd taken for just that end, the ones she'd become dependent on.

He found himself teasing her. "Don't let consideration for your table partner stop you from wiping it clean."

She chewed on without looking at him, spoke only when her mouth was empty and she was uncovering one of the simmering dishes. "Don't worry. I don't consider you at all."

Like its predecessors, that comment flowed with the bad blood he'd established. This time he realized what the spasm that shot through him was. Regret. If only...

But he of all people had no time for if-onlys. He wasn't just a man with his own emotions and convictions at stake, he was a monarch whose actions controlled the reins of peace in a whole region.

"You don't consider anyone at all," he bit off.

"By that you mean I'm not bowing to everyone's wishes without a word, don't you? What did you all expect me to do? To feel? To say? Oh, two more parents? Cool! The old ones aren't my real ones? Bummer. They lied to me all my life? Shame. All those hunky cousins are really my half brothers? Phew. Good thing I haven't lusted after any of them. I have to give up my life to get bartered in a political game to a boor? Whatever. Can I have a latte now?"

This was no laughing matter. But the way she'd delivered her parody, her choice of words, her sheer cheekiness, was irresistible. His chuckle overpowered him.

She sighed. "Glad you see the black humor in this 'situation.' It *is* what *sharr el baleyah ma yodhek* was coined for, a plight big enough that only hysterical laughter can do it justice."

He gave a grudging nod. "The revelations must have been a shock, I grant you that...."

She clapped in mock delight. "Ooh, can I frame your grant?"

He fisted his hands against the urge to lunge across the table and drag her over to him and willingly rose to her bait. "You can. I can even issue you a royal declaration for a more frame-worthy concession."

"Wow. You've grown generous in your old age. Don't splurge on those decrees and declarations, though. They might dry up on you."

"Can you by any stretch of your admittedly wildly fertile imagination see that happening?"

"Nah, this here Pacific would dry up first."

"This here Pacific has to take care of its own abundance. I have that of my decrees and declarations taken care of. As for you—" he leaned closer, his gaze sweeping resigned appreciation over her "—it's abundantly clear your own old age has been good to you." He raised one eyebrow. "If not to your tongue. I don't remember it being anywhere near this... forked."

That tongue came out to glaze those perfect lips, sending his hunger roaring to sample the moisture, drain it. "No? Are you sure your memory, once so reliable, isn't going?"

"My memory will be the last thing that dims in me, around the time I turn a hundred and twenty."

"You intend to deteriorate that soon?"

"Just being realistic here."

"Heh. You probably are, too. But one word of advice. In this constant gloating state over your superiority, don't drive while anywhere outside of Judar. You'd be apprehended for driving under the influence of a mind-altering high."

"What and whose purpose do I serve if I don't act on my superiority? You don't see a lion hiding his just so that other animals won't think him full of himself."

"A lion, huh? You're really stretching to fit the job description, aren't you? Lord-of-all-you-survey galore."

"You mean you don't think the shoe fits?"

"You mean you think *any* shoe exists to fit your figurative foot?"

"One must never give up hope."

"You mean you don't give hope decrees?"

"I don't currently have it on my subjects' roster, no."

"That must be why there's still hope."

"I'm working on acquiring its controlling shares. Enjoy wild, unregulated hope while you can..." He paused when her eyes stilled on him with a new intensity until he groaned. "What?"

"I'm watching for the moment you slip into that coma. I'm also debating seeking help or leaving you passed out on the floor."

Another laugh took him by surprise. Just as this whole meeting had. This tug-of-war of wills and wits had dragged him into its rapids, was so fluent, so unlike anything he'd had with her, yet somehow the same. Their conversations in the past had been about mutual pleasure, not one-upping each other with witty salvos, but they'd been perfectly matched, totally on the same wavelength, kindred in tastes and views and perceptions. And how he'd missed that.

But the mind that had housed all those qualities he'd craved had also been infested by vices that had appalled him…

Her voice brought him out of his unsavory musings. "But all macabre comedy aside, that's how you all wanted me to react, right? So you could move on with your plans without the inconvenience of pausing for a few minutes to think about how I'm grappling with my identity and past, plus your proposal to completely mess with my future?"

"I am pausing for a whole evening."

"Yeah, sure. You want to hear about how I'm coping. Your memory isn't going but gone if you expect me to believe that."

He pursed his lips. "We must leave the past in the past."

She imitated his expression. "How very convenient for you."

"It's convenient for both of us. For our future together."

She jerked as if he'd slapped her, flooding his mind with the memory of her similar reaction when he'd revealed to her the ugliness of his agony and madness seven years ago.

After a long, frozen moment, she rasped, "This was all fun and reminiscent of the sordid past. But let me set one thing straight. We don't have a future together. Our kingdoms will have to come up with another way to secure whatever they're hatching together. I'll never marry you, not for politics, not to save my life."

It was his turn to stiffen as the mind-warping disillusionment of the past crashed into him, blasting away all softness and the spell she'd been weaving—that he'd *let* her weave—on him.

She'd changed, all right. Not for the better, as he'd been fooling himself up till now. But into a vindictive harpy who'd send a whole region to hell to have her revenge on him.

He sat forward in his chair slowly, slammed her with his own rage and animosity. "This was my mistake, as it was in the past— being so civil and accommodating that I give you illusions about your importance. But in reality, you always served only one purpose. The difference now is that it's a worthwhile purpose for a change. And you *will* serve it. As for what you think or feel, it's time you realized that your emotions and identity, your past and future, *you,* don't matter. Not at all."

Three

Aliyah didn't jerk this time.

Not even when the fork clattered to her plate, fracturing the silence that had fallen in the wake of his barrage.

Time reversed like a screeching record. It came to a jolting halt at her last time in this mansion. Then it started to play. Memories of begging his valet to let her wait for him. Trembling on the way up to his bedroom. Gambling away the last of her pride. It hit Pause on his face as he'd issued his final threat. Then it all overlapped, merged with the same savage face now flaying her with his loathing.

Fool. Reason and self-respect lashed her, harsher than he could ever be. She'd been letting them slip away ever since she'd laid eyes on him again. They sneered at her now, at her flimsy struggle to slow down her headlong plunge under his spell. At the way she'd let him encroach on her senses, wiping her memory as he'd advanced.

After his initial shock—which she could only attribute to her changed appearance—he'd seamlessly changed tacks, scorching her with the appreciation smoldering in his eyes, the awareness in his vibes and the amusement in his expressions, his words.

He'd laughed at her barbs, volleyed them back without rancor, baring himself to her ridicule, appearing to enjoy it, had stopped trying to reciprocate the abuse that had soon ceased to be that, morphing into teasing instead. He'd lulled her into loosening her grip on her rage and memories.

Then he'd mentioned a future. Together. And reality had slapped her in the face. With the rush of recollections. With the realization that every second of this evening had been another undetectable maneuver of a master manipulator.

She'd groped for her resolve, said what she'd come here to say. And he'd decided it was more efficient to give up trying to coax her into submission and was now coercing her into it.

He leaned forward in his seat, magnifying his silhouette against the light radiating from the room, his face in the moonlight a hewn mask of inhuman beauty and coldness.

Then he spoke, his voice freezing her. "Now that I've made this clear, let me make another thing as unequivocal. This marriage is happening. That's not up for negotiation. I've only called you here to discuss our terms in the deal."

Her vision began to blotch. She inhaled a choppy stream of oxygen before it blinked out, heard her wavering whisper. "It's another hostile takeover for you, this so-called marriage, isn't it? You make no distinction between discussing one or the other."

He leaned back in his seat, relieving her of a measure of his influence so that breathing turned from a struggle to a mere effort. "For once we agree. Hostile takeover just about sums it up. You're hostile, and I am taking over."

"You've got that only half right. I sure am hostile. With the best and worst of reasons. Not that you, your imminent majesty, are the essence of friendliness. As for taking over, not in this life. In any other, you can take your 'deal' directly to whatever devil you worship, in whatever hell you'll end up in."

He sat forward again, probably to make sure she saw the glint of revulsion in his eyes before he grated, "I *am* taking my deal to the devil I have to deal with, *am* walking into the hell I have to end up in. Now stop aggravating the ugliness of the initiation rites of this hellish pact and state your terms."

She wasn't crumbling under his onslaught. She wouldn't let him shove her to the ground and walk all over her again.

Her scoff was still weak as she choked on his venom. "Have you gone deaf from the repeated injury of perpetually hearing only your own voice booming inside your head? I said in plain English there'll be no deal. You need it translated to something you understand better? *Mafee sufquh.*"

"*Lell assaf, es'sufquh mafee menha maffar.* To translate—regretfully, there's no escaping the deal, in case *you* no longer understand more than the rudiments of your mother tongue."

Indignation at the dig she'd heard a thousand times infused heat into her chilled bones, steadiness in her voice. "I'm as much an American as I am a Zohaydan, even if in reverse to what I thought. So don't play the turning-my-back-on-my-roots card."

His lips stretched on a silent snarl. "How about the turning-your-back-on-your-family card?"

"Oh, no, not that one, either. You don't know anything about me or about how it's been with my parents, not in the past when there were only two, and surely not now there are four of them. You have nothing to do with any of it, so don't you *dare* even have an opinion on how we all deal with it. Keep out of it and it'll turn out fine. The only person I'm turning my back on here is you."

His eyes narrowed, intensifying his menace. "I know far more than you so obliviously think. About you, and about what you put and are still putting your parents through. And though there's nothing I want more than to watch you leave thinking you've gotten your own back, I'm not letting you walk away."

"Aren't you going too far into the realm of irrationality to enforce your will? To put through this ridiculous 'deal'? *You* walked away from *me* calling me a depraved slut, if you remember. You'd make a slut your queen and the mother of your heirs?"

His gaze froze as silence stretched until it almost snapped every nerve in her body. Then he turned his face away, presenting her with the precision and power of his profile. Just when she thought he had nothing more to say, that she'd rested her case, his voice poured into the night, as deep and permeating.

"I remember one sunny day seven years ago, here in L.A. I was getting into my car when you threw yourself at me right in the middle of the street. After I pried you off me, you stalked me, did it again everywhere I went, not caring who saw your exhibitions or heard your shameless pleas, probably wanting to publicly embarrass me enough so I'd give you the chance to work on me again in private. If your memory is as intact as you claim, you surely remember what you said. Things along the lines of 'I need you' and 'I'll do anything.' Ring a bell? You make it sound as if I was insulting you, calling you what I did. Try to put yourself in the position of an unbiased observer and tell me, how would you describe your behavior as anything other than depraved and slutty?"

Had she burned to ashes? How had she not, after he'd shriveled her up once again with the memories? Of her own condition then, her actions, his reactions?

She finally rasped, "Depraved is right. As in out of my mind. But I'm very much in it now."

He turned back to her, his gaze the essence of ridicule. "A piece of precious advice. Drop the act. I had to tear your talons out of my flesh to make you let go. You want me with the same ferocity still."

A surge of scalding acknowledgment had her on her feet, quaking with mortification. That he was right, that her hated hunger had never died, the weapon he'd damaged her with. That he knew. Before any defense took shape in her mind, he rose to his feet, too, slow, measured, pitiless.

"In case you're preparing to launch into empty posturing and pretense, save it. I can feel it, coming off of you in waves. All this 'I'd rather die than marry you' is to goad me into giving you what you want, isn't it? A game of pursuit? With some reluctance and dominance thrown in? Go ahead, admit it and I'll promise to give you what you know will leave you gasping within an inch of your life with satiation, and let's move on to something important."

She shuddered with rage. At herself, at his unjust words and malice. Was this how people had arteries burst in their heads? She felt herself going numb, her tongue filling her mouth, swollen with the incoherent need to lash out.

Nothing came to her rescue. Nothing but, "You...*bastard*."

His lips pressed together for a moment. Then they spread on a heart-wrenching parody of a smile. "It's not me who is one."

She almost doubled over.

She didn't, stood there feeling as if he'd just punched through her, stared his cruelty full in the face. After all he'd done to her, she still hadn't thought him capable of such a level of heartlessness. Her mind emptied, her heart flooded. With the acid of desperation. For something to deflect the pain with, to send it ricocheting into his black heart, to not let him have the final word. Not when it was *that*.

But what could be enough to answer a stab through the heart?

She shouldn't have walked into his trap. Should have known how this would end. Shouldn't have taken him on, shouldn't...

Just get out of here.

She staggered around, felt the floor turning to quicksand, struggled not to sink into it.

Suddenly something sank into her—the fingers that an hour ago had barely touched her on the elbow and disrupted her balance and wrenched a response from her, that had once stripped away whatever control she'd developed before she'd met him. She wished they were violent. They were only inexorable in intent, cruel in effect.

He aborted her momentum, kept her on her feet, turned her around to meet his wolf's eyes as they flared with antipathy. "You're not walking out on your responsibilities like you have all your life. It's time you behaved like the princess you regretfully are. You will honor your duties and for once be of use to others."

"Use?" she threw at him, hating him even more for the quaver that robbed her pain of any retaliatory effect. "That's all you think people are for, don't you? To be used. Well, as you say, I had one use to you in the past, and damned if I'm ever going to be of any use to you again. It's not dramatizing to say I'd rather die."

"You think it's any kind of life for me to be forced to make use of you? Do you think I want to marry you? The woman I found out was too depraved to be even one of my sex partners? But I *will* marry you. For the throne of Judar."

Every word lodged into her with the force of an ax in the chest. And for the millionth time, the frustration, the sheer mind-consuming confusion reverberated inside her.

Why all this revulsion? All this fluency of abuse? All she'd ever done once was lose her mind over him....

And it was there again. Like the ocean, advancing on her with its endlessness and blackness, the tide of volatility. Her vision, her emotions began to distort, to fracture, the swirling black hole she'd once been unable to exit staring at her, pulling...

No. She would *not* let him do this to her.

She wrenched herself from his hands, spat, "You and your throne and your Judar can go to hell."

He seemed to expand, his hands fisting at his side. She knew that if she'd been a man of equal size he would have pulverized her.

Finally he ground out, "What about Zohayd? And your father and king? You probably care nothing if they go to hell, too, but before you consign them there, give it some thought. Think what you'll lose, if Zohayd is dragged into civil war."

"Civil *war?* What are you talking about?"

"The war that will break out in both our kingdoms if our union doesn't come to pass."

She stared at him as if he'd started talking a language she barely understood, shook her head. "Don't you think you're being far-fetched here? Zohayd is rock stable. You want to convince me that if a personal deal between you and my uncle…my fa-fa…K-King Atef falls through, Zohayd will go up in flames?"

His gaze was long and considering, the flames of his own fury banking. "So I'm being far-fetched, eh? You think anything less would make me come near you again, let alone give you access to my life, this time as my wife, to carry my name, my honor, my heirs? You won't take my word, just as you didn't take your adoptive parents' or King Atef's? When would you be convinced that our marriage is imperative? When rivers of blood run through both our kingdoms? When neighbors turn against each other, kill each other's children and blood feuds erupt to spread devastation for centuries? When our whole prosperous region turns into another war zone that breeds anger and hunger and intolerance and spreads its infection to the rest of the world? Or would you even then say, sorry, not my business? Just because you are a woman scorned, you'd send millions, entire *countries,* to hell?"

The images he painted, his conviction, suffocated her. She raised her hands as if to ward off a barrage of blows. "Please…stop. I—I— God…are you telling me the truth?"

"No, I project death and destruction for millions of people because it's fun."

"God…" She couldn't speak for a long moment, her throat feeling as if it were clogged with thorns. Then she looked at him through the film of moisture that manifested her dissolving control. "I didn't know—didn't realize the situation was anything like that. My unc—my fa…King Atef…he—he… Dammit! That medieval throwback! He said *nothing* like that. I know Zohayd and Judar are still tribal beneath their ultraadvanced veneers, but this is taking the entrenched stupidity of not including women in matters of state too far. He told me only that it was a political marriage, gave me the impression it was something personal between the two of you, as two monarchs. I…h-had no idea w-what was at stake…"

Then she could say no more.

Every muscle in Kamal's body bunched, pulled, contracted, until he felt as if his spine would snap and his skull would cave in.

Tears. Gathering in those eyes, rippling like ponds shaking from nearby explosions, magnifying the moon's beams, shooting them out in erratic flashes to blind him.

As she struggled to contain the weakness, stem the weeping, he felt her every tremor shudder through him, shaking him.

Ya Ullah, how could the sight of her distress disturb him this deeply, disarm him this totally, still? Had nothing changed? Was her spell unbroken? Or was it unbreakable?

B'Ellahi. What kind of king would he be if on his first and foremost act on behalf of his kingdom, he let his only vice, his clearly uncured addiction, take hold of him again, steer him?

He had to remember the times she'd wept for him when she'd been lying to him with every breath. The months her unbridled abandon had snared him when it—and the warnings that she was nicknamed Alley as in alley cat—should have cautioned him.

But he'd heeded nothing and no one, had thrown himself into an inferno that raged higher every day. If her mercurial nature and evasions had bothered him, she'd overwhelmed his reason with the pleasure she'd given him in every way, with her fervent protestations of love. She'd even had him agreeing that what worked—and spectacularly—was for them to keep on stealing scorching times together out of their busy and conflicting schedules.

Yes, she'd manipulated him to perfection. Until he'd showed up unannounced at her condo, unable to wait to see her and had been let in by one of the girlfriends who seemed to use Aliyah's place as theirs. And he'd discovered her stash of a drug he knew was abused for appetite suppression and as a stimulant.

It had all made sense then. Her hyperactivity, her thinness, her insistence on keeping her distance, and the hundred other details of unexplained reticence and secrecy.

But fool that he'd been, though anguished at his discovery, he'd still tried to make her confess her problem so he could offer her his strength, his support. But she'd denied drug use, ever.

Even with the blatant lie, he'd been so deeply under her spell, he'd only wanted to save her, though he knew from agonizing experience that addicts only plunged deeper into addiction until nothing of them was left, while they dragged everyone who loved them right along with them to hell. For a month he'd struggled to decide how to proceed, the indecision infecting him with reticence, too, which had made her even more eager for him—and increasingly more volatile. At last, with his decision set—to confront her and break the vicious circle she was prisoner to by any means necessary—he'd gone to her condo again. This time, he'd found a man there.

He still couldn't believe how far in her power he'd been that he'd refused to jump to conclusions. He'd told himself she hadn't been there after all, and this man could have been one of the friends she gave free run of her place.

But the man, Shane, had introduced himself as one of her American cousins…and lovers. He'd still accused Shane of lying. Shane had scoffed. With his barbaric ways and views of women, did Kamal think that a woman like Aliyah, free and capricious like the wind, could settle for him alone? Kamal might be an all-powerful prince, but Aliyah valued her sexual freedom above all. Why did he think she never agreed to enter his gilded cage, even fleetingly?

Kamal had left before he killed the man, but sensing Shane was jealous and probably trying to drive him away, he'd called Aliyah to get her side of the story, giving her every opening to tell him about Shane without accusing her of anything. She'd said only that she was spending the night at a sick girlfriend's bedside. Almost convinced that she'd given her backstabbing cousin the use of her place for the night, he'd still waited in his car, to make sure that she didn't come back. But she had.

Everyone had been right. She'd been a promiscuous lost cause.

Then she'd walked in here today, and he'd forgotten that. Had wanted to forget. Still wanted to. As he couldn't.

He had to brace himself against her influence. He wouldn't sweep her into his arms and comfort her even if his heart was bursting from the holding back. Now he had to get on with his plan.

He inhaled. "I'll suppose what you're saying is true. But if you didn't know before, you know now."

"B-but how? Why? What could be so important about a marriage between the Aal Masoods and Aal Shalaans all of a sudden?"

He gave a bitter huff. "It's heartwarming how involved you are in your region's internal affairs. I beg your pardon, your *half* region. I bet your abundant…roomies know far more than you about the situation between Judar and Zohayd at the moment."

Those mystic eyes glittered their indignation at him. "And that's another piece of misinformation in the sea of misconceptions that form my character in your mind. I live alone as I always have. I only ever helped friends by giving them a roof over their head when they needed one. And I'm a hermit when I'm preparing for a show with most of its paintings commissioned. I haven't been following the news and as I told you, nobody chose to enlighten me. Must have been their misguided way of being kind. Rather than dropping all bombs on me at once, they decided to space out the explosions for prolonged suffering."

She sounded so convincing. But then when had she ever not?

He exhaled his frustration at how she kept snatching resolve out of reach, made him struggle to grab it back.

"I'll pretend that's a good enough excuse for your obliviousness." He paused to gather the threads of the situation that had lead to this point. He hated recounting it, and to her of all people. But she'd asked. She didn't know. And she had to, as his future queen. He exhaled again. "When my father, the crown prince of Judar, died, and with our late king having no sons, leaving the succession to his nephews, the Aal Shalaans in Judar demanded their turn on the throne. They threatened an uprising if they didn't get it. An uprising that would drag Judar into civil war."

Though reddened and wounded, her eyes stained with disdain. "If you care for peace so much, why don't you just give it to them?"

"You think giving up the throne in a country that's made up seventy percent of Aal Masoods and tribes loyal to them would promote peace? Wouldn't exchange an uprising by the Aal Shalaans for one by the Aal Masoods, leading to the same end? Spare me your insights into a better solution for this catastrophe. If there'd been one, I would have gone to the ends of the earth, would have, as you so theatrically said, laid my life down for it. But there isn't. The one thing that will maintain peace now is introducing the purest Aal Shalaan blood into the royal house of Aal Masood's lineage."

She looked everywhere but at him, as if seeking an escape, and mumbled, "And why not go for the foremost Judarian Aal

Shalaan house for this blood-mixing ritual? Why is King Atef the one whose blood must provide the magic ingredient? He's Zohaydan, not Judarian, for God's sake!"

"You'll have to ask the Aal Shalaan genealogists that. They're the ones who decreed that King Atef has the purest Aal Shalaan blood in both kingdoms, from both sides of his family, for as far back as possible. Since he had no daughter that we knew of back when that was determined, it became clear it was a two-sided ploy. To throw the most powerful Aal Shalaan at us, and to corner him into giving in to their demands to help the Judarian Aal Shalaans in their quest to rise to the throne, something he'd already refused to do point-blank at the risk of having an uprising in Zohayd. Then King Atef discovered he did have a daughter, and you know what happened from then on. Now the Aal Shalaans have cornered everyone, including themselves. They can't go back in their decree, and King Atef's daughter—you—is what satisfies their demands. But in case we don't marry, they're very clear they'll seek their so-called right to the throne through less than peaceful measures, in both kingdoms, plunging both into chaos and dragging the whole region right along. Any solution other than our marriage is a lose/lose proposition. I trust you didn't forget everything about our region? You do remember how history went? How feuds start at the least provocation only to widen and engulf everything in their path?"

Silence crashed down again, as did the ocean waves as if in response to the enormity of his projections.

Her eyes remained riveted on his, as if begging for a repudiation, even a qualification. As they had seven years ago.

He'd had no idea he was that strong. To remain where he was, not to obey the clamoring instinct to crush her into his arms.

When he remained rock-still and silent, hope seemed to seep out of her. "It is that bad, isn't it?"

Everything inside him stilled. He'd thrown in her face his assertion that she craved him still. He'd been out to provoke her, to punish her for daring to remain *his* craving, his addiction. Now that dejection, that desperation in her eyes—could it be that this wasn't another manipulation?

It didn't matter. Manipulation or truth, only one thing was relevant. He told her.

"It's worse. We have a deadline."

"A deadline?"

Aliyah heard the quavering voice of the punch-drunk entity that seemed to inhabit her body.

Kamal, that forbidding stranger, only nodded. "In five days. The day of my *joloos* will also be our wedding day."

She felt as if she were going under, struggled to kick to the surface, to snatch one last breath of air. "There has to be another way, Kamal… We can't get married…we hate each other…."

He flexed his fists as he closed the gap between them. "And you'd be surprised how many kings have married queens they abhor for their kingdoms. But here comes another decree to ameliorate the horror. After you conceive a male heir, I won't touch you. After you give birth, I will divorce you."

She stared at him, *too much* blaring through her mind in a loop.

And he was going on. "The Aal Shalaans won't care after that, as you are only the instrument of securing the heir they want. Once that happens, everyone will get something out of this mess. King Atef will get Zohayd's continued peace, and I will secure Judar's throne and future. What do *you* want? State your demands, Aliyah."

"State my demands?" she panted, hysteria staining her voice, tumbling through her blood. "In return for being used like a breeding mare then discarded like a lame one? How about the royal jewels of Judar? I hear they're worth billions."

And if she could think straight, she would have feared him at that moment. His gaze boiled over with rage and aggression.

Suddenly all heat plunged into subzero reaches.

Then he only said a clipped, final, "Done."

It was then that Aliyah realized what the agony she felt at his every slashing word was.

Somehow, she'd never stopped loving him.

How had that happened? How had her emotions survived the injuries, the bitterness, the changes in her, the passage of time? *Was* she the depraved slut he believed her to be? Loving him even through the abuse? Or even because of it?

No. She'd fallen for him when he'd been incredible to her. So incredible, even his cruelty hadn't erased the memories. The image of the man she'd thought was her soul mate kept superimposing itself over everything that had happened afterward. Her mind and soul kept rejecting the proof of his words and actions, still looking for reasons for his change, for ways to exonerate him.

But she believed his words now, that things were as perilous as he'd described. And in a situation that big, what did her emotions and future matter?

He was right. They didn't. *She* didn't.

But no matter how insignificant she was to him, in all this she mattered to herself. Now that she'd realized the depths of her self-deception and weakness, it was up to her to quell them. So that his disgust and disregard didn't annihilate her.

But there was one thing she couldn't quell anymore. Tears.

She let them escape, inside and out. "What if I can't... c-conceive? What if you can't father a baby? What then?"

He grimaced. "You'd still keep the jewels, don't worry. But my fertility isn't in question. If you turn out to be infertile, that would be grounds for an easy divorce, even with our culture's constrictive royal matrimonial laws. Then I'd negotiate another marriage with the daughter of the second noblest patriarch of the Aal Shalaans."

"Just like that, huh?" She hiccuped. "Throw out the defective model and look for a functioning one…"

She stopped, at breaking point. *Just get out of here…now.*

He let her go this time when she stumbled around, following her silently to the door. Just as she groped it open, he broke his silence, his words lodging into her back again.

"Tomorrow you will be taken to Judar. As is our custom, I won't see you again until our marriage ceremony, but I will supply you with the list of things to be done, the rules to be followed." Then his voice dipped into bass reaches on a growl eloquent with everything that splintered her heart. "Don't disappoint me."

Four

"I would have given anything if only I could take it back!"

At the blurted-out declaration, Aliyah's gaze swept again over the woman sitting across from her. Judar's afternoon August sun was streaming through the western window of Aliyah's guest wing in the royal palace, turning the woman's hair into a blazing halo of undulating gold, striking turquoise beams off her eyes and drenching the perfection of elegant, chiseled features in a play of light and shadow.

Anna Beaumont was sure one beautiful lady.

It made Aliyah sheepish to acknowledge that the first thing she'd done when she'd laid eyes on her an hour ago was to marvel at their resemblance.

But there was no denying the fact that this woman could be her in blue contacts and a blond wig, with some aging makeup. Not much aging, though. Anna didn't look twenty-seven years older than her. Aliyah wouldn't have thought her a day above forty, a real good forty, if all that DNA evidence hadn't confirmed that Anna was her biological mother and therefore over fifty.

She wondered how King Atef had never noticed this.

But then, seeing a resemblance between his niece and the ex-lover he'd cast out of his life over a quarter of a century ago, especially with their opposite coloring, would have been a long shot.

When Anna didn't follow up her momentous declaration, Aliyah sat forward and poured another round of unsweetened jasmine tea from the heavily worked silver teapot into the hand-painted, blown-glass cups. The artistry behind their every line—more manifestations of the extremes of taste and affluence permeating the royal palace—roused the artist in her. It also sort of distracted her from the quiet, desperate feeling that she was sinking deeper into the quicksand of her situation, of Kamal's plans and decrees and existence.

She handed Anna the cup and held her eyes as they both drank in silence, her thoughts turning inward, going over the past two days.

Everything Kamal had said would happen had and was still happening like clockwork. She'd been delivered to her condo after their showdown, with that royal guard duet coming up to help her pack. She'd resorted to threats to make them refrain from folding her underwear and alphabetizing every item, had tossed them out only for them to ricochet back to her doorstep before the crack of dawn to accompany her to the Judarian equivalent of Air Force One.

Kamal was giving her the royal treatment all right. Imposing it on her more like. He'd sent her a clipped voice mail driving home that this was what she should expect from now on as his future queen. He'd elaborated on how she should receive her dues, mete out her responses with the poise, benevolence and grandeur befitting her impending majesty. Yes, he'd used those very words. And was evidently still conscious and in the best of health.

Finding no energy and no point in resisting his incursion

she'd let herself be swept away to her so-called future kingdom and installed in so sumptuous and extravagant a guest wing that it could have housed forty princesses. Then the list of things to be done that he'd provided for her had started to roll on.

First thing this morning was to have leisurely communications with three of her parents, informing them of her acceptance of the marriage of state and assuring them she'd play her part. With utmost attention to decorum, of course. As if.

She'd never treated those three in any way that wasn't grounded in love and respect, even when their actions had almost messed her up for good, but she was damned if she'd stand on ceremony with any of them. Kamal had to be satisfied with what she *was* letting him have—control over these countdown days.

She'd finished her conversations with her parents—who'd all been mighty relieved, she should add—and without missing a beat had headed to her dictated afternoon tea with her fourth parent.

Kamal had had Anna flown in from King Atef's court, where she must have been cause for some serious domestic disturbance. The queen—the woman who'd turned out to be Aliyah's stepmother—was a master of dissatisfaction, unreasonableness and conflict. Aliyah could only imagine her attitude now that she had real strife material on her hands.

And here they were. An hour into the long-awaited meeting. A twenty-seven-year-long wait on Anna's side, a two-week one on Aliyah's, which still felt like a lifetime. Aliyah thought she would have recognized Anna if she'd met her on the street. And it went beyond the resemblance. There was this unmistakable… connection.

She bet Anna had felt the same from the first moment, but they'd both reached an instant and unspoken agreement to test the waters first. She'd felt that Anna was agitated within an inch of her sanity at the enormity of the situation. She, on the other hand, was…comfortably numb. Too many enormous shocks could do that.

So they'd talked about Judar, Zohayd, compared royal palaces, weathers, customs, currencies, reminisced about L.A., which they'd both lived in and now seemed to have left behind permanently.

Then Anna had blurted out that fraught statement.

Seemed she was ready to wade in deeper.

Not that she was finding it easier. She let go of Aliyah's gaze, hers brimming as she stared down into her cup, choked out, "This sounds like so much exaggeration, like lip service, but I—I…I don't know what I can say that won't sound like…like…"

Aliyah put down her cup, invited Anna to look back at her with a gentle touch on her knee. "How about you say exactly what you're thinking? Feeling? It would save a lot of confusion. We've run out of small talk so I guess it's time for something big."

Anna nodded, her eyes reddening even more. Then she inhaled, whispered, "Do you resent me…too much?"

Aliyah plopped back on the couch and glided both palms over the cotton-silk pastels damask as she considered her answer.

Then she sighed. "Okay, I won't say I didn't resent this. I did. I do. But it's not you I resent. I don't presume to judge you. I can only imagine what drove you to the decisions you made, and that it couldn't have been easy or made your life better. When all is said and done, I can only say thank you."

Anna blinked. She couldn't have looked more stupefied if Aliyah had just told her she could turn into a bat at will.

Anna finally breathed. "You're thanking me? What for?"

Aliyah shrugged. "For not aborting me. It would have been the far easier, clean-cut route to go. And though my life hasn't been a bed of roses and doesn't promise to be, I'm still real fond of it. I wouldn't exchange it for oblivion. So…thanks."

Again, those blue-gem eyes surged with tears that tugged at the ones lying too close to Aliyah's surface now.

"I never dreamed…oh, God, that you would feel that

way…." Anna stopped, panting, then burst out, "*Do* you really feel that way?"

Aliyah gave her a tremulous smile. "One thing you will find out about me soon enough is that I go around saying exactly what I really think and feel. A very objectionable practice, I'm perpetually told, but at least you know exactly where you stand with me."

Anna seemed to lose all tension, melted back in her armchair. "I can never tell you how…how it makes me feel, hearing you say that, that you really feel it. I've lived with the guilt, the pain for so long. Then I find out you're alive, near your father, well and loved, and that I can see you. I would have settled for seeing you from afar, for being deservedly hated by you…but you…you… You're wonderful, so full of light and life."

"Full of light and life, huh? Now that's a new spin on things. To everyone else, I'm full of erratic energy and instability."

Anna looked genuinely taken aback. "How can anyone think that? I can't think of anyone who's less erratic and unstable."

Aliyah threw her head back on a self-deprecating laugh. "Oh, postpone your verdict until you've known me longer than an hour."

"I won't change my mind a year or ten years from now. Things like that are the first thing one feels from others. You're energetic, vivacious and from what I've heard, incredibly creative, truly independent and have the strength of your convictions. And yes, you're unpredictable, but I don't need more than the past minutes to realize it's in the best of ways. You clearly do what's right rather than what's accepted."

Aliyah lips twitched. "Wow, that's quite a testimony. Can I call on you next time I have to fend off accusations of irrationality? Hmm…I do what's right rather than what's accepted. I think that will be my new slogan, Anna…." She stopped, bit her lip. "Uh…is it okay if I call you Anna? I'd feel weird if you wanted me to call you Mom or something."

Anna surged forward, eagerness spilling from her tremulous

smile. "As long as you call me at all, I'm happy for you to call me anything that feels comfortable to you."

Aliyah's smile grew. "Anna feels comfortable."

In answer, Anna's smile faltered. Aliyah felt she could see into the older woman's mind, that she thought she wasn't entitled to this level of ease with the daughter she'd given up.

"Listen, Anna, as you said, time isn't an issue here. What happened is in the past, so let's leave it there and move on. Now. I don't want to observe a period of appropriate awkwardness. If you want to know me, if you want to be a part of my life, then let's start now. What do you say?"

Anna looked like she'd burst into tears before she nodded vigorously. "I do—I want all that. Oh, God...how could anyone ever think you erratic and irrational?"

Aliyah stilled. The call of blood, Anna's willingness to do anything to atone, to know her, be there for her now that she'd found her, surged inside her. For the first time in her life, she felt she wanted to, *could* share her secret.

She took the leap. "When I was six, my teachers couldn't interest me in anything in school, couldn't even get me to sit down. I was always listening to voices and seeing whole worlds inside my head and telling everyone who'd listen—and even anyone who wouldn't—about them. I was almost diagnosed as autistic, but I was too curious and could talk anyone under the table. Therapists had to label my condition so they settled on ADHD."

Distress crept into Anna's face. "This is my fault...you inherited those tendencies from me. I was always too hyper, too awake, too quick, too something or other. It was what drew Atef to me, and I think what ultimately put him off—apart from the fact that he had to marry for his kingdom."

Aliyah shook her head. "I bought into the psychobabble for a long time, but I no longer do. Who's to say what's 'hyper' and what's not? What's 'too much' of anything? We're individuals who can't be quantified. They wanted me to conform, and when I didn't they decided there was something wrong with me, tried to fix me and almost ruined me for life. They misdiagnosed me, put me on prescription drugs, kept increasing the dose to get the effect they were seeking until, for the next ten years, I was a zombie."

Anna gasped. "Oh, my God…oh, Aliyah, I'm so sorry."

"Yeah, me, too. I feel like I missed my childhood, that it passed before me while I watched it from behind a distorted barrier."

"Didn't your—your parents realize that?"

"Yeah, but not for many years. At first they were so relieved when my teachers—the ones who'd started the whole thing— started saying I'd become an exemplary student, citing that as proof of their insight into my so-called condition. Later my parents kept attributing my subdued state to puberty. By the time I was fourteen, they could no longer fool themselves and tried to wean me off the drug. I went ballistic. I don't remember what happened exactly, but I think I tried to commit suicide. They gave up, put me back on it. I didn't know what was going on. I trusted them and took my medicine like a good girl. Then when I was almost seventeen I overheard a very enlightening conversation. They'd long realized I'd been misdiagnosed, or at least that I had a severe reaction to the drug—to both taking it and trying to get off it. And I decided to take matters into my own hands, kick the habit that I realized had been controlling me all my life."

A tear raced down Anna's cheek. "How did it go?"

"To hell. The mental and psychological version. I was an addict, and I went through every kind of withdrawal. I think I went totally insane for a while."

Aliyah fell silent as her heart stampeded as if she were in the throes of one of those episodes again. Putting her ordeals into words was both cathartic and exhausting.

A long time later, Anna hiccuped, whispered, "But you're okay now. You have been for many years."

The urge to comfort her surged within Aliyah, came out on a fervent "I *am*." Then she felt compelled to be as honest about the rest. "Though I can't call getting shoved into a marriage of state to the last man on earth I ever wanted to see again 'okay.'"

The tear trailing down Anna's cheek became a stream that splashed on the hands upturned helplessly in her lap. "Oh, my God…it's all my fault again. Everything I am, everything I did affected your life so profoundly. It's still hurting you, changing the course of your life where you don't want it to go. I kept thinking maybe I don't need to feel so guilty, since everything was turning out great for you, especially since I saw your g-groom and thought him incredible…"

Aliyah huffed the breath she'd been holding. "You and every female on the planet, Anna. That doesn't make him human."

Anna looked as if she might have a heart attack. Aliyah wanted to reach out and comfort her. She curled her hands on the urge for a second then exhaled. What the hell. She was what she was. And one thing she'd never stop doing was comforting others in distress.

Anna jerked when Aliyah reached out and squeezed her shoulder, her eyes widening on such a mixture of surprise and hope that Aliyah groaned. "It's not your fault, okay? I may have thought that when I was still in shock and having an internal tantrum, but that's just too far-fetched. You didn't make the Aal Shalaans into grabby bastards, and you didn't make Kamal a ruthless one."

"You're making me feel even worse, being so kind."

"I'm just honest." Aliyah smiled, prodding her to smile back, to lighten the mood. She had enough heartache in her future, she couldn't take any now. "One way to look at things is that it's a good thing you had me, or two kingdoms would be on the brink of civil war right now. I'll go down in history as the chess piece that defused the whole mess. Not many women can boast such a pivotal role, even if it is, alas, a passive one. Still, most women marry for far, far less and do nowhere as much good. We can even say that your relationship with—let's call him King Atef, since I can't get around to calling him Dad, either—has been preordained, so you'd have me and I'd be the peace chip."

Anna's smile trembled, as did her voice. "That's certainly one way to look at things."

"Makes everything sound so much better and worthwhile, doesn't it? How about we sanction it as the official version?"

Anna nodded, her eyes filling with a jumble of pain, relief and anxiety. "I never dreamed I'd cause anything like this. I didn't know who or where you were, then Atef found me and I let him think Farah was his daughter, when she's my…my…"

"Your adopted daughter. Your real daughter, really. Being your biological child doesn't make me that. I always believed a child is raised, not born."

Anna's gaze faltered. "And you don't want us to have any more than a biological link?"

She surged forward, put her hand on Anna's knee. "Oh, I do. Though I don't know if I can come to think of you as my mother. I already have one, whom I love, even though she let so-called experts mess with my life. But I know she did it out of an almost pathological need to see me healthy and normal."

Anna gave her a sad smile. "Then that is something besides you that I share with Bahiyah. I almost messed up Farah's life with the same pathological need."

Aliyah's lips twisted whimsically. "Hmm, another thing I have in common with Farah. Wow. I can't wait to meet her."

"She can't wait, either. But she doesn't want to impose on you."

Aliyah gave her a mock-wicked glance. "Oh, I'll impose on her. I have three days to get ready for the wedding of the century, as the list my 'groom' gave me indicates. I need all the eager-to-please people I can lay my hands on."

The sounds of powerful cars gliding to smooth stops tickled her ears as she spoke.

Kamal's cavalcade. She knew it. The king had come home.

She quirked an eyebrow. "Say—how about we stretch our legs?"

Anna nodded, swayed to her feet, smoothed her sky-blue skirt suit and fell in step with Aliyah as they exited through huge French windows to the enormous veranda leading to a dozen thirty-foot-wide stone steps and the wing's garden, an explosion of flowers and rare plants.

Anna, still bent on elaborating on the main issue eating at her, didn't seem to notice the cavalcade drawing to a stop at the palace's main entrance. "You're so willing to deal with the most awkward things, with your pain, so openly, and I have the feeling you can take on the whole world and come out the winner. Yet, with all your pragmatic approach, you haven't accepted this marriage as you claim, have you? You're feeling…trapped."

Pragmatic? This lady had way too much to learn about her still. But she'd gotten one thing right at least.

She *was* trapped. In a marriage without love or respect. But she should console herself it was also with a time limit. In nine months' time, if she proved to be a fertile little chess piece, he'd do an encore of his favorite trick and cast her aside.

Not much of a consolation when she thought of her track record. The first time he'd done that, he'd almost destroyed her. Any bets he'd succeed this time?

Aliyah heaved a huge sigh, nodded and stood straighter as Kamal stepped out of the middle limo.

He saw her the split second he straightened, his eyes slamming into hers across the distance.

In the next second anger radiated off of him like a shock wave.

Didn't like that she was letting him see her, did he? Going against the dictates of their culture and its unreasonable demands of decorum, its servitude to and belief in the caprices of luck and its evil influences. Supposedly if the groom saw the bride in the five days before the wedding, their marriage would be blighted with inexplicable incompatibility and strife.

She couldn't see how theirs could be blighted with worse than what they already had—ill will, bad blood and subzero expectations.

She held his gaze, came forward so he could take a good look at her. *Disappointing you yet, ya habibi?*

His imperious face and body filled with the answer, with the unmistakable intent to stride up to her and let her hear it, along with a few more decrees no doubt, maybe even a restraining order. She only made a face at him, tossed her hair and turned to Anna.

Anna gaped at Kamal for a moment before turning stunned eyes on Aliyah. "My. Oh, my. That was…*intense.*"

"Yeah, that's Kamal for you."

Anna shook her head dazedly. "I meant both of you. The vibes you generated were enough to send Judarian homeland security reaching for a nationwide red alert."

Aliyah let out a resigned laugh, glanced sideways at Kamal, found him still standing there, glaring at her, looking like the bronze colossus of a wrathful god.

If only he didn't look so…everything. And have a character to match. Except when it came to her. A shudder rattled through her.

Anna caught her gaze, concern showing in her heavenly eyes. "This marriage isn't just a hated duty to you, is it? You want it, yet you believe it won't work and you're…scared?"

While that was a simplistic way to sum up the mess, Anna had again cottoned on to her basic turmoil. She took a last look at Kamal, saw the promise of retribution for defying him, for flaunting his precious customs, written all over him.

Her smile was conceding and defiant at the same time as she sighed. "Witless."

* * *

"I like her already."

Kamal rounded on Shehab, glowering. Shehab only grinned at him, his enjoyment glaring, chafing.

"A woman who isn't intimidated by you, who can pull that face—*ya Ullah*, that *face*—on you, is all right by me. More than all right. She's a once-in-a-lifetime find. A treasure."

Kamal wondered how the international community would react if, during the countdown to his *joloos* and wedding, he engaged his smug older brother in a knock-down, drag-out fight. Would it really matter if they both showed up at the ceremonies with broken noses, stitched lips and black eyes?

He exhaled the surplus of aggression. He wasn't letting Shehab bait him. Aliyah had done too good a job of it.

She'd let him see her. And after he'd made it clear he expected not to see her until she came to him in her *zaffah*. He'd invoked customs when in reality he just couldn't deal with the added turmoil of seeing her again one second before he had to.

And he'd been right to stipulate that ban. His current condition testified to the accuracy of his projection that seeing her would mess with his coherence and control. He couldn't afford that now when he needed them most.

And Shehab, *alf laa'nah alaih*—a thousand damnations on him—was taking such joy in plucking at the last anchors holding his restraint in place, giving him a taunting, considering look. "But this isn't her reaction to a fresh exposure to you, is it? It doesn't feel like the outcome of one meeting. Her defiance of your incomparable powers of exasperation feels too…established. As for your reaction…*b'Ellahi*, it was *priceless*."

Kamal bared his teeth at Shehab before casting his gaze again where she was no longer standing. He still saw her in his mind's eye, as if her focus on him had left a brand that still sizzled.

He tore his gaze away, cast it to the stately spires of the innermost palace gates, which were flying the flag of Judar at half-mast in mourning for his late uncle, King Zaher.

The weight of responsibility pressed harder on his shoulders, the best cure for his personal upheaval. He exhaled, strode toward the expansive steps, taking in the palace in an inclusive glance. He felt he was seeing it for the first time.

The four-level soaring, sprawling stone edifice was a marriage of the cultures that formed Judar, its architecture a melting pot of their grandeur, each line, ornament and texture owing its design, method and philosophy to one culture or the other. Somehow Byzantine, Indian, Persian, Turkish and other influences conspired to form an Arabian whole, echoing a vast, rich and sometimes brutal history. The palace still owed enough to Western modernization to be a monument of today. And tomorrow.

It reminded him of Aliyah.

And it was his dominion now. The seat of his power. A power that combined his own global influence with that of the throne.

He scaled the steps faster, felt Shehab keeping up with him, his taunting gaze still burning the side of his face.

"What I regret is that I didn't catch it all in digital memory for the viewing pleasure of the coming generations."

Kamal shot him a sideways look. "You do remember your warning to me, when I was taking your beloved Farah's name in vain? You, too, have a perfect set of teeth to cherish and protect, if only to flash them like a fool at your enchantress. So shut up, Shehab."

"Is this a command, *ya maolai?*" Shehab all but wiggled his eyebrows as he called him "my liege." Then seriousness crept into his hard, noble features. "Is Aliyah why you think love affairs are destined for heartache and humiliation? Why you've been like a tiger with a festering wound these past years?"

Leave it to Shehab to fathom it all simply from watching him seethe across the distance at Aliyah. He *had* been like an agonized tiger since he'd cast her out of his life, his disillusion-ment becoming total intolerance of any human frailty. But he'd always been fair in his ruthlessness.

He hadn't been with her. Not two nights ago. He'd slashed at her with unforgivable things. The inferno she'd ignited inside him, physical and emotional, had obliterated control and judgment.

And he couldn't let that happen. The throne of Judar depended on him. The peace of the region. He had to keep Aliyah at arm's length emotionally, would join with her physically only to produce the vital heir. He couldn't let her overwhelm him again. As she could, so easily, so totally, if he ever weakened.

Shehab was going on. "I won't probe..."

"Oh, please do. Then I can have the pleasure of probing right back. Into your maddeningly, obliviously blissful face."

Shehab sighed. "If I thought it would help, I'd let you. You probably think I owe it to you for passing the throne to you."

"You talk as if you passed me a ball."

"I did my share of the running but had to leave the touchdown to you." Before Kamal turned on him, made *him* touch down face-first, Shehab raised placating hands. "But sports metaphors aside, whatever went wrong between you, Kamal, bury it. She'll be your woman, your wife and your queen. And she looks and sounds like your match. You must have felt enough for her in the past if it hurt that bad and affected you that long when things went sour. Focus on the positive, dismiss the negative. Treat her well and it can only circulate in a flow of goodwill and intimacy."

Kamal slowed as they passed through the soaring mahogany doors. "What's this? Did our mother leave you instructions to read me before I married? Or did you find this in a wife user's manual? Or an edition of *Domestic Bliss for Dummies*?"

Shehab threw his head back on a hearty laugh before his gaze turned penetrating. "I want you to be happy. You haven't been for a long time, Kamal. I don't have any information on the situation, but I do trust my instincts, my heart. Especially after they led me into what you so strongly object to, the deepest reaches of love with my incomparable Farah. I want the same for you."

Holding back his response, which would have been riddled with obscenities, Kamal picked up speed as they crossed the vast columned hall that sprawled underneath a gigantic dome. The transition from the glare and dry heat to the interior's soothing light and the coolness achieved by the palace's structure and building materials silenced him. That, and feeling that he was seeing everything through new eyes now that he would call the palace home. His and Aliyah's.

The sweeping spaces, the extreme opulence, the floors that looked like polished extensions of the palace's beaches, felt as unreal as the whole situation. And the man who'd been the cause of it all was at his side spouting romantic nonsense.

He finally shot Shehab a dagger of displeasure. "Thanks, but no thanks. I don't want to be in the deepest reaches of anything. I'll leave wallowing in the depths of blinding self-deception to you and Farooq. You especially, as a spare crown prince, have it really easy. No pressure, no demands. You threw the job of king in my lap, now leave me to do it right."

Shehab's gaze lengthened until Kamal felt he'd given him a total mind scan, documented every thought and evasion and struggle. Then Shehab finally wagged his finger at him. "Attitude."

Before Kamal showed him some real attitude, Shehab's gaze suddenly gentled. "Don't take the past into your future, Kamal. It serves no purpose but to poison your views, your very life."

"Ah, talking from precious experience now, aren't we?" Kamal scoffed as they halted in front of his stateroom and he sent guards away with a flick of a hand. "How preconceptions robbed you of appreciating to the fullest every moment of your plunge from the realm of sanity to life under your siren's influence?"

Shehab had the temerity to look moved. "Such an indescribable waste, yes. But a wise man learns from others' mistakes. Don't try them yourself just to find out for sure that they'll yield the same result. For they will."

"Your situation," Kamal spat, "as pathetic as it is, is nothing like mine, your mistakes in no way comparable to my alleged ones. *You* leave the past out of the future and bury your head in the sand. There's nothing more around here."

Shehab's gaze summed him up again, then he exhaled. "If you don't think you owe it to her, or to yourself, you owe it to your subjects. Forgive and forget, or you won't be the king they deserve. Or change your mind. Try it. It might turn out to be the best move of your life, letting go of preconceptions and bitterness."

"Watch it, *ya akhi*. You might one day overdose on optimism."

"I'll take that over doing so on pessimism any day. If the end is the same, at least I'd have the journey. Think about it."

Kamal gritted his teeth. "Yes, sage older brother. I'm in your debt for this pep talk. How can I live without your wisdom?"

Shehab looked around, then after making certain they were alone, smacked him on the back of his head. Hard.

Before Kamal charged him, Shehab bowed deeply then turned and walked unhurriedly away, chuckling. "Anytime...*ya maolai.*"

Five

"So...you're my sister, in just about every way, huh?"

Aliyah cocked her head as she avidly examined the woman with the most artless, most infectious smile she'd ever seen.

With hair in every gradation of bronze and gold, eyes the color of Judar's emerald shores and the rest of her an unusual blend, Farah had an atypical beauty, another thing they had in common. And she wasn't being smug here, about her own beauty.

Personally she'd never seen what the big fuss was about. But the world had had another opinion, at least the world of Western media and advertisement. That had valued her exotic mix so much they'd paid big bucks for the privilege of plastering it on their campaigns and products, had made her able to support herself without her family's money or power, and sponsor a dozen causes, too.

Farah was also clearly of mixed ethnicity, though which ones, it was even harder to tell than with her. Was that why Anna had adopted her? To remind her of the girl she'd given up?

Farah eagerly nodded. "Oh, yes. And I'm ecstatic about each and every one. Oh, God—I can't begin to tell you what the last couple of months have been like. I was living this no-expectations life, then I met Shehab. And as if that wasn't beyond dreams, this happens. It's still hard to wrap my head around it all, when I spent my life wishing for any sort of family. Now I not only have a sister who'll be my sister-in-law, too, but you're American—well, half-American—my age and you'll share the same residence."

"If you can call living in the palace a mile apart living in the same residence!"

Farah chuckled. "Yeah, we'll probably never bump into each other without a previous appointment."

Aliyah returned her smile, ignoring the spasm that constricted her heart. No reason to rain on Farah's parade, inform her that within a year she'd be out of there, one way or another. It wouldn't serve any purpose right now to say that her marriage to Kamal would have no resemblance to Farah's marriage to his brother, Shehab, which had been born of love and the willingness to sacrifice anything for the other.

A good thing she held her tongue, too. She would have hated to douse that blaze of eager happiness on Farah's face.

"I want to talk for days," Farah said. "But we don't have days. Not now. But after you settle down after the wedding—though I'll have to wait months for that—I'd just adore it if we fill each other in on our whole lives. I'd probably go blow for blow so you better stop me if I inundate you with redundant info."

Aliyah tried to keep her smile plastered on. "Oh, I'll talk you under the table the first available minute."

It wasn't only Farah's assumptions about an unending honeymoon period between her and Kamal that hurt, it was Farah's radiance that had Aliyah almost wincing. This was one woman whose name befitted her. She was joy—and overjoyed—indeed.

And why not? She was married to an Aal Masood god who worshipped anything she'd ever touched, was a bride of just two weeks and, from the way she kept touching her tummy, was considerably more than that pregnant. And she, Aliyah, was yet another source of happiness for her newfound sister.

Not that she begrudged Farah her joy. On the contrary. Farah was a guileless and untainted spirit the likes of which she'd never met before, and she knew that finding her would enrich her own life endlessly. But right now she felt like one raw, exposed nerve ending, and emotional emanations as intense and pure as Farah's were putting her in a seizure of distress.

Farah added another layer of agitation, touching her hand again as if she couldn't believe Aliyah really existed. "So— Mother said you can use my help, so here I am, reporting for wedding duty, totally and completely at your disposal."

Aliyah arched an eyebrow, attempted lightness. "You sure your husband would approve of such time-consuming devotion?"

Farah laughed, her eyes turning jade at the mention of her husband. "He's very understanding…since it's only for three days."

"Stress on 'days' here." Aliyah swung her eyes toward the door at the melodious, humor-filled words to find a classically beautiful, Rita Hayworth–type garnet-redhead with sparkling turquoise eyes and the most gorgeous baby girl Aliyah had ever seen hooked on her left hip. The tot was staring at them with extreme intelligence and interest radiating from her incredible golden eyes—eyes that could almost be Kamal's. Yes, an Aal Masood, all right. "If we venture into the 'nights' we'll have some very grouchy, all-Judarian, supreme Aal Masood males on our hands. And we don't want to risk that, do we, ladies?"

"Carmen! You're back!" Farah squealed, sprang up and ran to hug the other woman and kiss the baby before turning around to Aliyah with excitement spilling from her eyes. "This woman is *the* goddess of event planners. She whipped up a miracle of a wedding for me, from the ground up, in no time flat. All I had to do was jump into my dress and run to Shehab among a sea of perfection. You're so in luck that she came home in time to take over!"

So this was Carmen, the eldest Aal Masood brother's, Farooq's, wife. The one who'd started the domino effect of abdications leading to the throne ending up in Kamal's lap. Another woman emanating bliss. And a baby—who must be Mennah—who was clearly equally contented and secure.

"Even if Farooq didn't cut our trip short to come back for the *joloos,* you thought I'd miss having a hand in the wedding of the century?" Carmen smiled at Farah, rapport flowing between them. Then Carmen turned back to Aliyah. "That is *if* you want my busy hands there."

Aliyah groaned. "Will it do if I grovel for them instead of saying how absolutely wonderful it is to meet you?"

Carmen's laugh rang like tinkling crystal. "It'll do. Oh, boy, those Aal Masood brothers are always in such an indecent hurry to get married. Sure, they say they have all those world-shaking reasons for the mad rush, but it turns out they just couldn't wait to get their hands on us."

Farah giggled. "In my case, his hands *back* on me. Not that it was long in between, I capitulated within a day..." She stopped, looking appalled that she'd revealed such details, a blush blazing under her perfect tan.

Carmen placated her. "I may have held up for sixteen months in between, but not one minute of those was up to me, mind you."

What the hell, Aliyah thought. *Let's join the confessional.*

She sighed. "I hold the record, then. It's been seven years. Not my doing, either, mind you."

Carmen chuckled again even as her gaze turned mind-reading. "The Aal Masood brothers are a breed of their own, all right, and they can be ruthless. But there's no one better, or fairer."

Farah nodded eagerly. "And from our experience, it seems a

bumpy start leads to incredible things. You can only imagine, with your start so much bumpier, how incredible it'll be for you."

Aliyah bit her tongue. Not a good idea to start this relationship by telling them to speak for themselves. For her, a bumpy start would lead to a crash. And Kamal had been ruthless *and* unfair, in the past, and now.

But then he'd always operated on a different morality system from the rest of the world. Now his basic sense of right and wrong would probably no longer even resemble that of lesser mortals.

Carmen's smile widened, her intention to steer back to lighter zones evident. "I hold another record, though. I had less than forty-eight hours from marriage proposal to the ceremony…uh, if you can call that cocktail of imperious command, fait accompli decision and inescapable coercion Farooq hit me with a proposal."

"You, too, huh?" Aliyah shook her head. "Guess I should console myself that it runs in the family."

"Seems so. The good news is, it bodes well for Kamal turning out as incredible as Farooq—" Carmen looked at Farah "—and Shehab." She looked down at Mennah, who was squirming to be let down. "Now, Mennah, how about saying hi to your new auntie? She'll be your queen, too, little princess."

Aliyah stood up, stiff and shaky as she approached the curious baby. "Hi, Mennah. I'm Aliyah. Don't listen to your mom. She's being very nice and all, but I just want to be your buddy."

Mennah let out an excited squeal and threw herself at Aliyah.

Carmen laughed out loud. "Welcome to the family, Aliyah. Mennah throwing herself at you—what we call the 'Mennah Test'—is the surefire indication that you're an Aal Masood now."

Tears filled Aliyah's eyes as she hugged Mennah. She hoped they'd think it a natural reaction to a baby with a cuteness factor of a million, when she was in the grip of upheaval over entering a world of enormous responsibility and the poignancy of projecting when she'd have her own baby.

All that was accurate. But as the resilient little body filled her arms, the scent of healthy baby her nostrils, she thought only of when she'd have her own baby…only to lose it. To Kamal's cruelty.

Clearly Farah didn't suspect a thing, but Carmen seemed to realize there were agonizing depths to Aliyah's ready tears.

Aliyah wasn't surprised. She sensed Carmen was a far more complex soul than Farah, one whose scars had deepened her insight, not to mention tempered her spontaneity, if only in comparison to Farah's. Carmen *seemed* open, but Aliyah sensed that she could be impossible to read if she wanted to be, something Aliyah doubted—no, *knew*—Farah was incapable of.

Carmen now took her baby back from Aliyah, smiled gently at her. "So…what do you have in mind?"

"Mind? What's that?" Aliyah groaned again as she wiped tears with both hands and both women laughed. "But in lieu of a mind, I have a list. Provided by my groom-to-be. Just looking at it made my eyes cross and my mind cease to function."

"Sounds like Farooq's brother, all right. But I think Kamal is even more…uh…*elaborate* in his opinions of how the world should revolve. And more insistent it follows them to the last detail."

"You think right. Still think you can help? Still want to?"

A determined, excited gleam fired the depths of Carmen's gemlike eyes as her smile widened. "You mentioned a list?"

"There is still time for you to change your mind."

Aliyah's lips twitched at her mother's quietly frantic words.

Not with humor. There was not much to smile about with the ceremonies starting in half an hour. She was at the breaking point with trying to keep up a bright front for everyone's sake.

To escape having to answer, she sauntered off to the full-length mirror, watched the very tall woman coming nearer. It felt as if she were looking at a stranger.

Her time as a model had seen her at her most unanchored. She remembered the whole thing as if it had happened to someone else, the memories vague and unreal. She never connected the image in ads, the woman strolling down the runways with herself.

Since she'd stopped modeling, she'd been looking at herself in the mirror only for unavoidable self-maintenance.

Now the woman in the mirror didn't look anything like the one she remembered from those days. She looked nothing like the one who'd looked back in the mirror a few hours ago, for that matter.

It had to be the outfit. As a princess and a model who'd worn the best that designers had to offer, she'd still never seen anything that came within a hundred miles of it. And to think it had been one of a hundred choices that had been presented to her, every one the epitome of creativity and grandeur. She'd chosen this one, a sarilike creation that had appealed to her on all levels.

Her gaze glided down its magnificence, marveling at the fusion of styles—Indian, Arabian, Persian and Pakistani being foremost among those—the blend of exquisite fabrics— handmade bobbin lace, chiffon, georgette, crepe and *jamawar* silk—that combined to turn it into a masterpiece.

The corsetlike top had a plunging décolleté, narrow shoulder straps and a concealed front zip. It reached a few inches below breasts that looked the fullest she'd ever seen them, exposing a lot of midriff between it and the skirt that hung low on her hip bones. The *tutreez* embroidery was on a level of beauty and precision she hadn't known human hands were capable of. Each stitch and motif that heavily embellished the top from neckline to scalloped hem was something she could spend hours just gazing at, marveling at the sheer genius and patience of those who'd brought it into existence.

She fingered one of the patterns at the top of one breast, marveled again at how no motif was repeated, how every unique one flowed to the next in a symphony of form and harmony. The weave of gold and bronze threads, the placement of tiny mirrors, the spray of silver and rainbow sequins, the arrangement of matte and glossy ribbon, appliqué, pearls and what she'd been informed were actual gems. She must be walking around wearing the equivalent of a few hundred carats of semiprecious and precious stones.

Her gaze slid to the *lehenga,* the fitting, flowing skirt of heavy-weave silk *jamawar* that echoed the top's embellishments and caressed her thighs and legs as it flowed around her like something alive with a will of its own.

The *dupatta* veil was a chiffon material that, while also heavily embellished, seemed to defy the laws of nature, flowing like wings one moment and wrapping around her protectively the next.

"You can still wear one of the other dresses."

Her mother's insistence had her teeth grinding. She'd been louder this time, bringing looks from Anna, Farah and Carmen. Aliyah wasn't allowed even the freedom of choosing her own wedding dress?

Aliyah gave half a pirouette, looked her mother's reflection in the eyes. "I look good in this one."

Her mother's agitation rose a notch higher. "You do, but…"

"I rest my case." Aliyah turned around to the ladies. "Okay, it's time to put on the tons of accessories I'm to lug around."

One of the items on Kamal's list was a very specific instruction that she was to be covered in jewelry from head to toe.

As Farah and Anna rushed to comply, her mother rose, approached her, urgency written all over her. "I do feel it isn't in the best of taste, let alone advisable…"

"Mama, *kaffa. Hada orssi.*"

At Aliyah's admonition of *enough, this is my wedding,* Bahiyah jerked as if she'd backhanded her. Aliyah's tears surged at the spasm of pain that racked her mother's face.

She lunged at her, contained her in a fierce hug. "Sorry I snapped at you."

Her mother pulled back, shaking her head, her eyes brimming. "No, no…you're right…*ya Ullah,* it's a miracle you're doing it at all. I'm just afraid of the repercussions, and with you… so…so…ah, *ya habibati*… I can't see you like that again."

Like what? On the brink of another plunge? She looked that bad? As bad as she felt?

She brought her mother's gaze back to her with a gentle touch. "I'm not like that again, okay?"

And that was the truth. She was suffering from nothing like her old rootless havoc that used to toss her wherever it pleased. This agony had roots that reached down inside her, branched out to encompass her hopes and self-worth, crushing both.

To have Kamal and never to have him, to be intimate with him again this time knowing that loathing for her filled his heart and mind, to feel it turning every touch into a scar, to wait in dread until she conceived, to feel his child growing inside her, to know how it would all end, with her pushed out of both their lives…

She gritted her teeth against the rise of bile, gestured toward the others, indicating their approach to her mother. "Stop worrying, Mama, okay? *Please.* I'm fine. It'll all be fine."

Her mother didn't look at all convinced, but had to let it go. On one hand, she knew there was nothing to be done. On the other, the women converged on Aliyah to accessorize her, and she seemed to decide that the best course was to join in.

Aliyah stood there accepting their eager help, her role shrinking to yay or nay the pieces of jewelry they presented to her from that treasure box Kamal had sent her. His late mother's.

It was another custom for the groom to give his bride jewelry that belonged to his mother, if she wasn't there to bestow them herself. It had nothing to do with the *shabkah,* the gift that the groom "nets" his bride with, making sure everyone knew she was spoken for, that she'd be "held" for him. This was a matter of imparting a part of the most precious thing the woman of the house had—her jewelry—to the new woman who'd join the household.

Aliyah's mind whirled at the choices. Though she'd been born royal, her mother, a very modern and practical lady, had never been one for extravagant stuff, had raised her with the same mentality. She'd surely never modeled anything from the same galaxy. But this wasn't time to advocate a ban on personal items with prices rivaling the distance light travels in a year.

She ended up choosing a five-piece set reflecting Judar's rich heritage and affluence. The central piece was a twenty-four-karat gold *kerdaan* necklace that started in a choker and rained down her back and front, almost covering her cleavage, with cabochon pastel gemstones ensconced among a design made up of arabesque calligraphy and interlaced geometric shapes that all managed to end up being five-pointed, to ward off the "evil-eye."

The other pieces were earrings that dangled down to her shoulder blades, a *jhoomer*—a head ornament fixed to her right temple—a *haath panjaa*—a ring bracelet that covered the back of her hand and ended in a glove ring that covered her middle finger—and a *teeka,* a hair ornament that hooked with an intricate chain to her hair at the back of her head and came forward to dangle its tasseled, five-pointed medallion over her forehead.

Next came the *ghawayesh*—bangles that covered her right forearm up to the elbow—and a *kholkhal,* an anklet that jingled above her left foot every time she moved. Kamal had been specific about the latter. Pinning a bell on her like a cat? Afraid she'd pounce on him while he wasn't looking?

She was staring at herself as Farah and Anna enthusiastically added the last touch, pinning the *dupatta* to her hair, when an eruption of bone-jarring thuds made her jump.

She whirled around, her numbness falling away like shed leaves, leaving her shaking like one. "Wh-what…"

"That's the traditional way a *joloos* is announced," her mother rushed to say. "An explosion of sound heralding the new monarch's era. You don't know, since you haven't lived through one."

"I have now." And Aliyah couldn't believe how eager she was to experience all of it. Stupid moron that she was, her heart was tangling in her chest with anticipation of seeing Kamal as he claimed the throne.

If only she could see it from afar, then disappear so that she didn't have to endure the torture of the sham of a wedding and the so-called marriage that would follow. But she couldn't, and while she waffled here, she could miss his *joloos*.

She turned to the others. "Let's run and catch the spectacle!"

Farah whooped in excitement, and Carmen and Anna looked very relieved that they wouldn't have to miss it waiting on her whims.

It was only Bahiyah who didn't share the enthusiasm. "In Zohayd it isn't allowed for women to attend a *joloos*. I'd think it would be the same in Judar."

No kidding. Aliyah turned to Farah and Carmen. "Your husbands say anything to that effect?"

They both shook their heads, but Carmen said, "Maybe it didn't occur to them we'd want to, or even have time to since they knew we'd be busy with you to the last moment."

"Maybe, but you know what, I don't care. I'm the queen, in a couple of hours' time anyway, right? I say we attend this. If there's any trouble, just say I ordered you to. Or I can go alone."

"Oh, you won't." Farah chuckled. "I'm dying to see this!"

With that settled, Aliyah streaked out of the wing she doubted she'd ever set foot in again. From tonight on she'd be in the king's apartments, which she'd heard had been totally overhauled for a king in his prime. She wondered what that meant. What kind of renovations did a king "in his prime" need?

She'd find out soon enough.

The others followed her through the spacious corridors, had

to explain to their ladies-in-waiting, who'd been waiting outside to take their place in *zaffet al aroos*—her bridal procession—that it wasn't time for their participation yet. She looked back at them, blinked at the cream-colored collective dream of exquisite womanhood they all made in their matron- and maid-of-honor gowns.

She heard Farah shouting, "God, what's making all the noise? It doesn't sound like cannons, more like thunder."

"In Zohayd, it's five hundred drummers belting away in unison on all the traditional percussion instruments," Bahiyah supplied.

Aliyah winced. "Sounds like Kamal went for five *thousand*."

"He just might have." Bahiyah smiled tremulously, trying to be supportive, but clearly agitated that Aliyah was doing this.

"If you want to know what's making all the noise, sounds like *mihbajs*," Aliyah explained to the others, who were always avid to learn about their men's culture and grateful for any insider insights she provided. "In the Bedouin days, they were huge wooden grinders. Pounding them is supposed to scare away evil spirits. But from the volume of the sound, I'd say the bulk of it's being made on *tobool*, which are large African-like drums. All the tambourine-like instruments seem to be present, too. The huge *mazaher* and the smaller *doffoof.* Not the smallest *reg,* though, since I don't hear the jangles."

"Oh, those will be used in the *zaffah*," Bahiyah said. "Since it's a more festive and less weighty ceremony."

Less weighty, huh? Guess it was. Not to her, though.

They were now a few dozen feet from the doors leading to the southern gardens, where the wedding would take place. The doors where he'd wait for her, to escort her to the *ma'zoon,* the cleric who married couples, in their *kooshah,* the place they would sit during the festivities, secluded from all others.

She stepped outside and was assailed by everything. The glare of the declining sun, the dry heat of the dying day, the rich tang of the sea, the hot scents of the desert, the potent sweetness of a hundred fragrances from the dozens of varieties of fruit trees and flowers. But it was his aura that reached out and embraced her as powerfully as he once had in his arms. And that when she could barely see him.

He was exiting the palace grounds to the mile-long path to Bayt el Hekmah citadel. The *joloos* ceremony would take place in its ceremonial hall, as all major royal state events did. That was why the late King Zaher had built his palace here, to be near it. It seemed Kamal was heading there on foot, with his deafening procession in tow. And even with hundreds of guests and media people in pursuit, his towering form stood out, swathed in pitch-darkness, absorbing light. She only noticed his equally towering brothers behind him at their wives' excited squeals.

Her own tiny procession stopped at the end of the grounds, where guards informed them they were banned from going farther. So her mother had it right. Women need not apply.

She dealt with their ban in two succinct sentences, but could still have only the princesses accompany her.

Looking back in apology at Anna for leaving her behind, she rushed after Kamal's procession.

The ban was repeated at the citadel's gates, but with anticipation almost bursting her heart, she had guards scattering out of her path with two words this time. She knew how to play the royal card if she had to. And she was sure playing it now.

She had only one goal. To see him the moment he sat on the throne. She felt nothing around her as she sailed through the impossibly opulent edifice that had stood the test of six hundred years undisturbed, a testament to Judar's grandeur.

Then she was standing at the doors of the gargantuan ceremonial hall and sound turned off. Everything ceased to exist.

Kamal. He was facing the door, in floor-length *abaya*, high-collared top and pants fitted into matte leather boots, in all-black to signify his assumption of the mantle of power. A supernatural being descended on earth to rule, to conquer.

His brothers had their backs to her. Then Shehab extended to him *sayf el welayah,* the sword of succession, of power, a viciously magnificent weapon. The shallow curve of its single-edged steel blade absorbed the omnidirectional light, reflected it back in blinding flashes, the handle an alloy of precious metals inlaid with gems. Kamal went down on one knee, held out his hands palms up to receive the burden, the privilege.

The moment it landed in his palms, Aliyah groaned as if under the same weight. Which she would have shared for real, if their marriage wasn't a contingency tactic with an expiration date.

Then Kamal lowered his awesome head slowly, kissed the blade.

Aliyah's heart lurched, as if those lips had landed on her most intimate part. As they once had. As they would again.

Or maybe not, now that it was all about impregnating her, not pleasuring her or taking his pleasure from her....

The toxic thoughts spilled inside her until he rose to his feet, then in a measured motion, raised the sword over his head.

He stood there, a force of nature dominating the whole place with his overpowering presence, a king born, destined to rule over all others, by merit as well as by divine right.

And as if unable to do anything but obey his influence, the whole attendance rose to their feet, heads of state from the East to the West, with King Atef and his crown prince and other heirs—her brothers now—foremost among them. Then there was the Tribune of Elders of Judar and every head of the Aal Shalaan houses.

When he had them all waiting for his next action with what had to be literally bated breaths, he lowered his arm, held the sword out perpendicular to his body, the tip pointing heavenward.

Then he spoke, his voice a bass rumble that traveled in the citadel's foundations, reverberating until it rattled her bones with his intent, his conviction.

"Fe hada al yaum, yaum joloosy alal arsh, oqsem b'Ellahi an ahkom shaabi bel adl, wa obadir'ruhmuh, wa akoon aqwa haleef le holafaa Judar, wa aata a'doww le a'da'ehah."

In this day, the day of my sitting on the throne, I swear by God that I will rule my people with justice superseded by mercy, be the most powerful ally to Judar's allies, and the most merciless enemy to its enemies.

And she knew. These were not vows that had passed through the lips of other kings. These were his. And he would abide by them to his last breath. He was maddeningly intractable that way.

He sheathed his sword in its golden, bejeweled scabbard, hung it from his six-inch worked-bronze belt. Then he spread his arms.

Her heart gave a leap that almost knocked her off her feet. Feet that tingled, ached, with the need to run. To him.

And she couldn't even *imagine* the magnitude of her stupidity. This wasn't an invitation to her. And she shouldn't want one. She *had* to enter this marriage, do her part, exit it, no emotions. If she wanted to exit it at all with anything intact.

Her nails still dug into her palms to keep herself from moving as she watched his brothers come forward, embrace him before kissing his right shoulder, then moving to stand by him, one at each side as the heads of state came forward to congratulate him.

She vaguely heard Farah and Carmen sighing over the sight the three brothers made together, before chuckling at how everyone struggled to reach up to embrace Kamal, deciding that those who had it easiest were the tribal heads who only had to stretch up to his shoulder in the only form of salute allowed them. He, of course, wasn't bending to accommodate anyone. Typical.

Then all the congratulations were over and Bahiyah informed them Kamal would now perform the *joloos* for historical records.

Sure enough, he gestured for all to resume their places. His brothers diverged to stand by the throne, an intricately carved, gilded work of art that she wanted to get her hands on to study, resting on a platform of mosaic marble with the engraved alabaster wall behind it rising sixty feet before the imperial Ottoman-style domed ceiling took over. Kamal scaled the steps toward it, the command radiating from his every step transmitting to her own nerves and muscles until she moved forward without volition.

At the top, he turned around in a controlled sweep, then, pushing his scabbard aside, he sat down on his throne.

At that very moment, his gaze slammed into her.

He hid it well. Perfectly. The stupefaction. It was undetectable. To all but her, she'd bet.

But he was beyond stupefied. He'd turned to stone as if he'd met Medusa's stare. Was it that she was here? Or was it her choice of wedding outfit? Or both?

He'd have to live with it. She'd ticked off the rest of his list. But she hadn't been about to stay away like a good little female and not witness this. She also hadn't been about to wear something chaste and act the virgin his bride was supposed to be.

Not when she'd ceased to be one in his bed, in his arms.

Six

Kamal would have keeled over. If he hadn't turned to stone.

Only Aliyah. Only she had ever done this to him. Only she had ever wrenched reactions he couldn't control, couldn't handle, from depths he hadn't been aware he had until her. Only her.

He'd felt her. Every step of the way here. Every second as he enacted the rituals. And he'd kept telling himself he was imagining it, was being obsessive, that he'd been feeling her a breath away, her scent whiffing in his nostrils, her shadow merging with his all through the past days when he'd been certain she was on the other side of the palace.

But she was here. Shrouded in the darkness of the hall's entry. Obscured. And still he saw nothing but her.

She'd witnessed the *joloos,* all of it. He knew it. She'd gone against every custom, broken every rule. Became the first queen—queen-to-be—to see her king's *joloos* firsthand.

And that wasn't the extent of her trespasses. The measure of her transgressions.

Black.

She was wearing black.

He'd specified his demand. Not white, since that was the color of mourning in Judar, but pastels. To signify purity. A bride was supposed to come pure to her groom in Judar. Most of all, to Judar's king. He'd specified the range of golds. To worship her coloring, to echo the shades of her hair and eyes.

But she'd worn *black*. The color of power.

And only their region would get her message. The rest of the world, watching the ceremonies on global live-feed, would believe she was mourning having to enter their marriage.

She probably counted on both interpretations.

Heat erupted in his head like a geyser.

She was doing it again. Breaching his defenses, invading his focus, compromising his position, this time during his life's most momentous occasion. During Judar's.

He wouldn't let her disgrace him, taint her image as his queen. He would have her taken back to put on another outfit. No, he'd walk out of here and go tear it off her sin-inducing body and put her into a suitable one, any other, in any other color…

Suddenly the heat roiling through his head splashed down his body and dissipated, a tide of calming realization filling its vacuum.

This felt nothing like the past. She hadn't interrupted his *joloos,* had watched it from the shadows. And while it was unheard of, that wasn't the behavior of a woman who didn't think about or cared nothing for the consequences of her actions. So why had she done it?

Had she wanted to witness this, such a landmark in his life, in Judar's history, her new home? Why? When neither of them mattered to her in the least? Or did they? Did *he?*

Whatever the answer was, yet another thing was different. None of her actions during her pursuit seven years ago had been borne of defiance, but rather desperation for attention. But that outfit—that was an out-and-out challenge.

And—*Ullah yel'anoh,* damn him, he *loved* it.

This was what he wanted, the only thing he could abide. An equal. A lioness. Giving as good as she got, never lying low, never saying die. Someone to keep him enmeshed in the game, unable to blink or risk missing a move, lest he be outmaneuvered.

He could think of her in nothing but black now. Could think of nothing more flattering. More fitting.

No. He wouldn't change what she'd done. Literally not for the world. Its approval was the last thing he wanted. He certainly didn't need it. Not in this. His only need was standing right there, her eyes on him even across the distance that turned her to a tiny doll, the only eyes he'd ever wanted to caress him, to devour him, reversing his paralysis, supercharging every nerve.

He could barely contain the ferocity of the need to jump to his feet, hurtle through the crowd, haul her over his shoulder and storm off to wherever he could devour her. Somehow he managed a semblance of calm, of sanity as he rose to his feet, stepped down from his throne, gesturing for the attendance to rise, all the time his gaze fused with hers.

The gathering of the most powerful men on the planet parted for him. He felt Farooq and Shehab following him as he passed through them, almost felt his brothers' merriment slapping him on the back as they, too, saw Aliyah. Yes, indeed. This would be an endless mine of ribbing for the next half century.

And he didn't mind. Didn't mind at all.

His heart quickened with each step nearer, as if it would outrace him to where she stood. He felt his lids growing heavy with the weight of lust, his lips filling with it, his palms tingling with all that he intended to do to her.

Everyone turned to follow him and saw Aliyah, no doubt realized who she was. A buzz spread like fire in dry tinder, the drone of hundreds of whispers circulating astonishment and amusement. The bride was wearing black?

Yes. His bride was wearing black. Would remain wearing it.

Let the world run rampant with speculation.

He was almost running himself, was dozens of feet from her when she bit her lip, dropped her gaze and swung around. Her companions hurried after her, looking back at him, each with a look to suit her character.

Those damned sirens of his brothers' had expressions to mirror the ones that no doubt adorned their husbands' faces. But it was the mix of apology and entreaty, of dread, in Aliyah's mother's eyes that gave him pause. She feared his reaction to her daughter's trick, feared he'd...what? Punish her? *Harm* her?

From the woman's distress it was evident that she thought the worst. She'd clearly misinterpreted his urgency.

He had no time for affront at her assumption that he—Judar's king and a knight of the Aal Masoods—would harm any woman, let alone his bride. And if something whispered inside him that he might not have harmed Aliyah, but he *had* hurt her, he ignored it. He hadn't even paid her back for a fraction of the hurt she'd inflicted on him. And then, he couldn't have hurt her much. Being hurt required sobriety and sincerity, both qualities she hadn't possessed then.

But that wasn't the issue here. Bahiyah, a princess of Zohayd, King Atef's sister, the aunt of men he respected—the three Aal Shalaan princes who would become his brothers-in-law—and most of all his mother-in-law in an hour's time, was still turning back every second step with the same fear seizing her face.

He had to defuse that fear, stem it at once.

He smiled at her. Then he winked for good measure.

The woman gasped, almost stumbled.

He smiled again, gestured. His *kabeer al yaweran*—head of

the royal guard—came rushing to his side. "See that your queen and princesses don't walk back to the palace grounds."

The man streaked away, had a limo screeching by the ladies' side in under two minutes. Before Aliyah reluctantly got in, she looked back, electrifying him again before she ducked inside.

His strides widened as the limo zoomed away. If it weren't for the hundreds of people and cameras in his wake, he would have put his record-holding long-distance-running ability to good use.

She'd hurled down the gauntlet after all, had left it up to him to give chase. And he would oblige her. How he would.

Let the games begin.

One hour later, as the sun disappeared from the skies, leaving behind an ephemeral masterpiece of incandescent hues on the twilight's horizon, Kamal was waiting to escort Aliyah through grounds that Farooq's woman had turned into a reproduction of the most lavish setting of *One Thousand and One Arabian Nights*.

He stood by the garden's southern entrance as the *zaffah* music segued into the traditional songs, anticipation reaching critical mass.

Then she appeared at the far end of the entrance hall, followed by her bridal procession. She glided across the floor, her majestic figure reflected in the mirrored marble, head held high, eyes staring into nothingness, every undulation of her ornate, black-swathed body a testament to the grace of a model-born, a female to overturn monarchies. Then she saw him.

She almost stopped. Anxious at his reaction? Good. He shouldn't be the only one with chaos reverberating in his bones.

Then, under his avid gaze, her model programming seemed to kick in, her steps gaining that poised prowl of a woman used to admiration and above caring about it. Insane wishes gnawed at him, that this wasn't a prison of duty they were entering know-ingly, where only torment awaited, that this was a marriage born of love. Everything that wasn't written in the fates. Not for him. Not with her. And if not with her, then never with anyone else….

All thoughts evaporated and his heart rammed his ribs.

At Bayt al Hekmah, she'd been shrouded in shadows. Here, as she neared him, the superb light exposed everything.

She looked as if she hadn't tasted food in days. The memory of her past fragility, that it might be returning, had bile backing up in his throat. And her fragility seemed worse now.

Before, she'd been hyper. In the past few days, she'd been confident, stable. Now…now she looked—*felt*—haunted.

And he could no longer evade the admission. No matter her defiance, she wasn't goading him. Not now, not before. She'd only been trying to stand up for herself. She truly hated this.

Something thorny expanded inside his chest, the pain it inflicted bringing him face-to-face with another fact.

He no longer hated her. He craved her. Beyond insanity. He refused to ponder what else he felt. Whatever it was, it was all irrelevant. Only one thing mattered.

She was his bride. No matter why or how or for how long. And he'd take her. He'd wallow in her until he was sated. He'd surrender to the hold she had over him until it was no more.

Maybe then he'd be free of her.

Decision seeped through him with the clarity only she had ever robbed him of. He let it order his thoughts, play on his lips. Then he extended his hand to her.

Aliyah's feet almost stumbled over each other again.

She'd expected Kamal to drag her back to the palace to be stripped of the offending black, midriff-exposing outfit. But once she'd arrived at the gardens, she'd only been informed she was to perform the agreed-upon *zaffah*.

Now he was standing there, an avenging angel from the realm of oriental fables, his pitch-black *abaya* spreading over endless shoulders, cascading for miles to his ankles, billowing around him in the twilight breeze like a shroud of mystery, of menace.

Not that he needed wrappings or settings. Kamal was the personification of both, of the might and wealth of this kingdom, of the best and worst of its deserts and seas, of the inescapability of the fates, for both Judar and her. The man she still loved in spite of the lessons of experience.

And from the moment he became her husband, the countdown to the moment he ceased to be that would start. If that wasn't the best reason ever to stop loving him, she didn't know what was.

He remained on the other side of the threshold she had to cross in symbolic consent of entering into a new life with him, his eyes fixed on her face, his body facing her, with head held high, feet planted apart and arms hanging by his sides.

Then he suddenly raised one hand, spread it in invitation.

But it wasn't *that* that had her almost falling flat on her face, that blocked out the deafening *zaffah* rhythm, the voices raised in congratulations of her incredible match, enumerations of her assets and those of her groom and well wishes for a future filled with offspring, what filled her head with white noise.

It was his smile. The smile of a predator. Not one bent on the kill but on the hunt, the struggle. Before a ferocious mating.

Before she could wrap her head around it, she'd reached him, found herself giving him the hand he'd imperiously asked for.

Then she was floating beside him into a waking dream sundered by a thousand flashes through the tamed oasis Carmen had turned into an *Arabian Nights* replica. No genie would have done better.

Grandeur enveloped them. Lavish traditional decorations came into focus as twilight deepened and the grounds blazed with countless Arabian lanterns hanging from a tapestry connecting the abundance of palm trees to the columns and arches of the gigantic tentlike construction whose roof was made of alternating strips of bunched masses of organza and the night sky. The sky that would barely know darkness before it blazed again with the full moon.

She kept her eyes everywhere but on the dark force walking beside her. On the cameramen rushing before them, on the hundreds of tables arranged in rows in a huge *C* with its opening leading to their *kooshah*, the stage he was leading her to in the massive clearing the tables were arranged around.

The stage was built of Arabesque woodwork, covered in red-rose petals, with two low-backed gilded thronelike chairs facing each other across a square table, a backless chair between them where the *ma'zoon* awaited them.

She felt Kamal raise his hand, and the music stopped at once. Her ears whooshed with the silence, the panic that followed.

Somehow she kept walking, or maybe he just swept her along in his orbit. She barely realized she was passing among hundreds of people, or that Farooq and Shehab were now walking behind them. Then she was scaling the petal-covered steps and walking across the stage. At her chair, Kamal squeezed her hand, bent his head to her in invitation to sit down. She managed not to plop down in her chair in a nerveless heap. He descended into his with an economy of grace that belied his size and mass.

"Aliyah, *e'teeni yadek.*"

She would have jerked if she could. The only thing that moved in her now were her eyes, slamming up to find him leaning forward in his chair, his forearm resting on the table.

"We're arm wrestling?"

She realized she'd said that out loud only when she heard the deep chuckles coming from Farooq and Shehab. Kamal's smile only deepened, its sensual promise bordering on threat.

He took her sweaty, limp hand, entwined it with his with their thumbs opposing, murmured for her ears only, "Later."

She was gasping as the respectful *ma'zoon* came forward

along with Farooq and Shehab, the two required witnesses to *katb ek-ketaab,* the writing of the book of matrimony.

Holding her eyes, Kamal dipped a hand inside his *abaya,* produced a pristine while silk handkerchief monogrammed with the Aal Masood family crest, handed it to the *ma'zoon,* who placed it over their hands, placed his hand on top and started to recite the marriage vows for each to repeat after him.

The moment the *ma'zoon* described her as *al bekr ar-rusheed*— the consenting adult virgin—she almost pulled her hand away.

Kamal seemed to anticipate her reaction, tightened his grip, his smile singeing her as he mouthed, "Temper."

She dug her fingernails into his hand below the handkerchief. *Here's temper for you, you bully,* she wanted to spit.

He only bit his lower lip in blatant enjoyment, his eyes growing heavier, sending a rush of response scalding through her.

She couldn't believe it. What was wrong with her? Were her responses malfunctioning so bad that he could arouse her here, now?

The *ma'zoon,* oblivious to the tug-of-war beneath his hand, kept on droning the vows he must have recited hundreds of times. She grudgingly repeated them after him. They weren't romantic vows, more like agreeing on the terms of a business deal according to a predetermined set of rules that were supposed to work for everyone. Which was very appropriate, and as sobering as a cold shower.

Then the man came to the end where he made them both repeat the part about agreeing to marry *Alas'sadaq el mosammah bai'nanah,* on the terms they named between them, and she was at a loss. Was she supposed to say something in answer to that?

Kamal squeezed her hand before he unlocked their hands, let his nails trail along her palm, making her core convulse. He watched her reaction in satisfaction. Harsh satisfaction.

The *ma'zoon* removed the handkerchief, started writing in the book of matrimony, documenting their marriage. After he asked for their signs and seals, then Farooq's and Shehab's, and offered congratulations, Kamal nodded to him, dismissing him.

She made to move, but Kamal gave her a look that kept her in place. What? Wasn't this part of the ordeal at least over?

He rose, walked away between his brothers till he saw them off the stage, then raised his arm.

Dozens of drummers launched into a hot rhythm on *darabukkahs,* vase-shaped hand drums, as they came running among the rows of tables to converge and form a path leading to the steps of the stage.

In seconds he was standing above her and her hand was back in his. Then she was choking on surprise as she ended up against him, his hand splaying beneath her *dupatta* against her bare skin.

"What?" he murmured as he caressed her. "You can wear this and send out the compound message that you are no virgin, one who mourns our marriage and one who's challenging her husband's power, when he is a king, no less, and I can't let the world see that our relationship didn't start after the *ma'zoon* sanctioned it?"

She felt her nerves short-circuiting. "I thought public displays of intimacy are a no-no in Judar, like in Zohayd."

His gaze lodged into her cleavage, felt as potent as his fingers, his tongue and teeth once had. "Oh, they are. But I'm sure everyone will excuse me, will even be cheering me on as I show you who's boss in this marriage after your blatant flaunting of their dearly held values. They'll even dismiss the nonvirginal black as the uninformed choice of a westernized bride. You've been declared to the whole world as *al bekr ar-rusheed,* after all."

She was about to blast him with something when the drummers, who'd been keeping a steady rhythm, suddenly launched into intricate, escalating patterns that wrung a storm of applause from the crowd. The uproar rose as a line of men in ornate black-and-gold costumes came running amid the path of drummers and up the stage, each two carrying a huge treasure chest.

Dazed, she let him pull her to the middle of the stage, where the men were going down on one knee, placing the chests in a side-by-side row. Kamal nodded to them and they opened the chests in unison. Aliyah stared. And stared.

She'd thought she'd seen every form of extreme affluence in her life. She'd seen nothing. Nothing compared to the content of these chests. What must put the content of the cave of the forty thieves or the treasures of Solomon to shame.

These had to be the jewels of Judar.

Kamal pressed her into him with a formidable arm, an even more formidable erection digging into her side as he lowered his lips to her ears and whispered, *"Mahrek, ya aroossi."*

Aliyah stared up at him. Had he said *Your dowry, my bride?*

The memory of her scathing demand and his lethal consent detonated in her mind. She lurched. He'd thought…he'd really thought she'd been serious? He was really giving them to her? Thinking she'd accept them? The freaking jewels of Judar?

She tried to squirm out of his hold, but he put his lips to her ear again as he waved for his men to close the chests and carry them away. "Smile. And wave to your guests, show them how happy you are for receiving the biggest *mahr* in history."

She found herself doing as he said, smiling and waving at the now standing, clapping attendance as she almost ran by his side through the drummers and all the way to their *kooshah,* another stage surrounded by polished brass pillars and screens of the most amazing craftsmanship and canopied in ethereal drapes of gold and bronzes that undulated in the evening breeze like living beings.

He seated her on the bronze damask couch, came down beside her, close—too close.

He gave another signal, and a *rababah*—an instrument that produced a unique and versatile string sound from a single string of horsehair—started a rousing melody, heralding the start of the festivities. It was soon joined by gusty, high-pitched, double-reed *mizmars* and the more evocative single-reed *naay* as the stage they'd written their *ketaab* on was dismantled in minutes.

The moment the clearing was empty, hundreds of men in desert robes poured in waving gleaming swords, followed by hundreds of women with waist-length hair in vibrant, heavily embroidered ethnic dresses. Drummers joined in as they formed facing queues and launched into energetic dance routines.

She sat staring ahead, drowning, in his nearness, in the hyperreality of it all, trying to shut him out of her focus. It should have been possible with that mesmerizing spectacle unfolding before her eyes. And dammit, she *should* be enjoying it, if only on account of it being a once-in-a-lifetime experience, one that so many people had poured such talent and beauty into.

Was she damned to keep on letting him ruin everything?

Suddenly he leaned closer, whispered in her ear, "Just let go, Aliyah. Enjoy this now."

She snatched a look into his eyes, every hurt she'd ever suffered rushing to hers. She felt rather than heard him groan. Then with a touch so gentle it had everything brimming, almost spilling over, he turned her face away and toward the display.

Trembling, unable to bear his suffocating nearness, she rose, wobbled to the edge of their *kooshah*.

She hadn't taken two half-decent breaths when Kamal was suddenly surrounding her, his fingers sliding up then down her exposed arms until his hands reached hers. Just as she felt he'd electrocuted her, he entwined their fingers for a moment before raising her hands and putting them together.

His lips caressed her ears as he murmured, "Clap if you find their efforts pleasing, *ya maleekati*. They're dancing for you."

She twisted her head to look up at him, ended up resting it on his shoulder, felt again the unsettling, alien and immensely satisfying feeling of being dwarfed, encompassed. Another thing only he had ever made her feel.

She tried to shake her head. It only rolled on the daunting muscle padding of his shoulder. She moaned. "They're not pouring out their talents and skills as if it's their last performance for me. They have this tiny matter of wanting to please their new king on the world-shaking day of his combined *joloos* and *orss*."

His eyes sharpened for a moment before they turned assessing. "Can you have forgotten so much about our region, *ya jameelati*? Or has your parents' commuting lifestyle seen to it that you were never in Zohayd long enough as a child and a teenager to fully assimilate how the region really works?"

He could say that. As a child and teenager, she hadn't been in this *realm* enough to realize how anything really worked, most of all herself. But she would *never* hint at the subject with him of all people, the epitome of control and stability. Better that she just let him believe his own interpretation. She nodded.

His eyes melted with a lava-hot indulgence she couldn't account for, that almost had her reverting to the liquid state. "Let me educate you, then. In our region, *el orss,* the wedding, is all for the bride. *El arees,* myself here, is just her escort on the day when all come to pay homage to her."

She huffed. "That's my main beef with weddings. And honeymoons. They sound like such a sucker deal to me. You get one night 'when all come to pay homage' and a brief time of mandatory bliss, then—wham, you're dumped into the humdrum life of being just another married couple."

He looked down into her eyes, surprise tingeing his. "You know what? You're right. People do mark their lives with finite milestones. Then, once they achieve them, they drift on in inertia, never doing what they want to do because they believe the time is past. But that's 'people.' You think I abide by any of those rules?"

No. She'd thought that he must play with a different deck of moral cards. But then, that wasn't exactly true, either.

"On one hand," she said, giving him an assessing glance, attempting the impossible task of not finding more details to salivate over, "you sure invent your own. But you always had that split-personality disorder I suffered from, even if mine was the mild syndrome, having never been an active member of my royal family. You were at once totally free of rules, yet somehow the most bound by them, by others' expectations and demands."

"Were you always this insightful, *ya maleekati,* or is this maturity's contribution to your character?"

She tsked. "*I* won't ask if you were always this condescending. On memorable occasions, both past and present, you were far worse. But I will ask this—were you always this evasive, or is it the diplomat in you, strutting his stuff? Wait, don't answer. It'll be another evasion. You become a diplomat of your caliber by always swerving to new territory to confuse issues."

"You make it sound as if a diplomat's purpose is by necessity something reprehensible." She grimaced, and he swept his hands over her bare midriff, gathered her back into him, his arousal a steel shaft against her back, making her lurch. "But I evaded nothing. I admitted it all by admiring your insight. As a tycoon of global power and far-reaching humanitarian and diplomatic objectives, I forged my own rules, yet had to abide by their letter while at the same time struggling to never let them cross those of Judar. Now that I'm king, I am at once unbound in power, yet thoroughly bound by responsibility."

She stood there, stunned, not only by the throbbing in her core that was escalating to pain, but also by the conversation they were having, that he was sharing this with her, that he was almost making love to her in front of thousands of people, even if he'd prohibited cameramen from coming near their *kooshah* after the preliminary shots of them in it for the record.

She was leaning on him, pressed into him, looking up at him as if drugged, when suddenly a storm of applause erupted.

Shehab and Farooq were striding to the clearing, spotlights following them.

"And here's another performance in your honor," he murmured.

Farooq and Shehab came to a stop in the middle of the clearing, shook hands then unsheathed their swords. They started sword-fighting to the music, escalating in ferocity and difficulty, treating the crowd to a masterful show of swordsmanship until they had everyone on their feet in a standing ovation.

At last, among constant cries for encores, they stopped, sheathed their swords and beckoned. Farah and Carmen almost flew to their sides as the music picked up into a beat that could make stone dance and the dancers flowed back, formed intricate formations around the royal inner circle of four.

Kamal swept her off the floor. "Come, let's join them."

She struggled to find her feet, squirmed out of his hold. "Oh, you go right ahead. I'm busy working on a headache."

"If you come and dance, I'll let you hold my…sword."

She met his taunting eyes, swerved to his daunting… swords. Then she gave up, croaked, "Only if I get to…wave it around."

In answer, he pounced on her, had her running in his wake until they were in the middle of the dancing formation. The crowd roared. The two dancing couples, the singers and dancers escalated their enthusiasm. He smiled broadly down at her, prodding her to move along with him. She watched him, his complex steps and accompanying body moves, the memory of similar dances coming back, rushing to her feet and body until she was moving with him to the primal beat, to the haunting, raw music, her heart keeping tempo.

And she found herself transported into another realm where nothing existed but him. Only his eyes, dominating her, luring her, inflaming her. He moved with her as if he were connected to her on the most essential levels, moved *her* as if it was his will that powered her body, his mind that ruled her thoughts.

It could have been an hour, a lifetime, before the dancing came to an abrupt end, to the vocal disappointment of the crowd.

Kamal raised his hands in placation, indicating there was more to come. Then he unsheathed his sword, the sword of kingship, went down on one knee before her, offered it up to her.

The crowd again stormed in applause as the heart that had long resided in her throat hit the top of her head.

She looked down at him, on his knee, looking up at her with something in his eyes that so painfully reminded her of the way he'd once looked at her. Pure survival kicked in, made her quip, "Passing on the job, already? But you've been king for only a few hours and all you've done so far is gesture and dance."

His smile flashed, riddled her vision in blind spots. "You only get to hold it for a while. To…wave it around. *If* you can."

She gave him a withering look, excitement replacing everything, bubbling in her system as she gripped the incredible handle. She lifted the sword. Heavy. Real heavy. Hence his condescension. She'd better get a two-handed grip on it.

She did, quirked her eyebrow at Kamal as he rose to his feet. "You're not afraid I might…wave it around…the wrong way?"

He chuckled at her implied threat. "In the direction of my head? Or is it somewhere a bit below waist-level you're thinking of? Or would either be the 'right' way, in your view?"

She gave him a look of pure condescension, stepped away.

Then without further ado, she performed an intricate swashbuckling routine flawlessly. All through, she could have cut through the silence with a saw. Through Kamal's amazement, too.

She finished her routine, lowered the sword, took the stance of someone waiting for a score she knew to be perfect.

Kamal's guffaw rang out, and only then did a rumble of

approval spread through the crowd, followed by stunned applause. These people hadn't heard of women's lib yet?

Instead of taking his sword back, Kamal remained standing there, shaking his head. "*Sayafah baad*…a swordswoman, too." On another laugh, he turned and beckoned to Farooq, who at once understood, threw him his sword. Kamal caught it smoothly, turned to her, waved it in arcs of challenge, excitement blazing from the twin suns of his eyes. "*Zain*, give me all you got."

"*Ghali wet'tulub rekhees.*" She rolled her shoulders, swung the sword over her head as she made a full turn and ended up facing him, in battle position. "Or is it the other way around? Cheap and the request is precious?"

"Cheap?" he teased, clearly having no intention of letting her goad him. "When I just gave you a few billion dollars' *mahr?*"

"You mean your *family's* jewels? Remind me to be impressed by your generosity when it's with your own assets."

He threw his head back and laughed as he circled her, a knight summing up his opponent, a predator his mate. "Oh, I'll show you generosity with my own…assets."

The crowd had gone wild from the moment they'd realized what they were about to witness. Now the music thundered to battle rhythms as they faced off, king and queen, in an unprecedented performance, an exhibition duel to end all duels.

She made the first strike. Kamal blocked it on an oblique sword, swept around, his robes billowing around him like a magician's cape, struck back. She felt him holding back, curbing his power. She spun and struck, hard, showing him he didn't need to. Exhilaration blasted off of him in breakers, dueling with hers as he threw himself into their clash, until she felt every hurt and prejudice evaporating in the inferno of excitement. Her passion raged unchecked, colliding with his with every meeting of their swords, the sparks they struck alight with the momentousness of destiny.

Then in one lunge, he caught her, disarmed her, molded her to him. And suddenly the drummers went wild.

"What are they doing now?" she panted. "Going into a frenzy?"

He sheathed his sword, threw the other one to Farooq and clutched her harder to him. "These are the drums of the deflowering."

"The…*what?*"

"You heard me."

Then he swept her off her feet and into his arms and cut through the cheering crowds.

Seven

The beast inside him roared.

It wouldn't be held back anymore. For seven long years he'd been keeping it on a spiked leash that had enraged it to madness.

This. This flesh. This spirit. This tempest of a woman. Her. It demanded her, would have her. And it wouldn't have her slow or gentle. It wanted her, *had* to have her, fast and ferocious.

And she wanted it, too. All the way she'd clung to him, her eyes engulfing him whole, her breathing as erratic as his.

But it was when she'd moaned, "Is this the fastest you can go?" that he'd thundered orders that had emptied his path, emptied the palace around his apartments in a five-hundred-foot radius.

He now exploded inside with her cleaved to him, not even noticing the exertion of carrying her and almost running through a mile of grounds, endless steps, then through the maze leading to his sanctum sanctorum. Where he hadn't set foot before.

He didn't even stop to see if the customizations he'd ordered had been installed, to his specs, or at all. He needed a bed.

He didn't find one. This wasn't even a bedroom, but an antechamber. The door that led into another room, maybe the bedroom, maybe not, looked too far away. And the beast wouldn't be held back one more second. It broke free.

He swept around, took her to the nearest erect structure, dimly realized it was the door they'd just come through, pressed her against it, put her on her feet and crashed his lips down on hers.

Her cry tore through him when their mouths collided. He could only grind his lips, his all, against hers, no finesse, no restraint. The need to ram into her, ride her, spill himself inside her, drove him. Incessant moans filled his head, high and deep, his and hers, as if in profound suffering. And he was, in agony. Her flesh buzzed her response beneath his burning hands.

He rumbled it all to her, the insane hunger, the intention to devour her, finish her, now. "*Abgha aklek, akhul'lussek, daheena.*"

"*Ella, ella, daheena*—yes, *yes*…now…" She grabbed his hands on a whimper and sank her teeth into them, suckled his fingers.

He snatched his hands away on a growl, felt as if they were not his to control as he struggled out of his bronze belt and sword and let them clang to the floor. He snatched at her top, mercifully found the front opening, the need to feel her flesh, the pressure to demolish the barriers between them becoming purple bursts clowding his vision.

Ya Ullah—was he having a stroke?

Not before he had her again. He could die after he'd had her again. It had been so long without her—so long…

He raised her up and she arched against the door, her breasts a desperate offering, her hands behind his head sinking further into his sanity, speeding his descent into oblivion.

He opened his mouth on her engorged flesh, took what he could of her ripened femininity, feasting on her feel and taste. He raised her skirt in uncoordinated moves, spread her legs around his hips. She thrashed, clamped around him, her moans distressed. His distress as deep, he held her with one arm, reached between her legs, pushed aside her thong, opened her folds and shuddered, on the brink just gliding his fingers along her fluid heat, blind with the acuteness of her response, with the blast of hunger.

He drew harder on her nipple as two fingers rubbed shaking circles over the knot of flesh where her nerves converged. He felt her stiffen, pant, gritted his teeth, anxious for the music of her release, hoping he wouldn't suffer permanent damage hearing it.

She came apart in his arms, magnificent, abandoned, her cries sharp talons lodging in his erection. He barely freed himself, anticipation so brutal his grip on consciousness was softening.

He fought back to focus as he brought the thighs that had melted off his hips back around him, growled as her moist heat singed his erection, even as her heavy-lidded gaze did the rest of him. His fingers dug into her buttocks and her breasts heaved, her hardened nipples branding his raw flesh even through his clothes.

As if through a long tunnel he saw her swollen lips quivering in her taut-with-need face, heard words, her voice. "Drums…still pounding…waiting for you to…"

He couldn't let her finish. He drove up into her, incoherent, roaring, invading her all the way, overstretching her scorching, living honey. And she engulfed him back on a piercing scream, consumed him in a velvet inferno, in her clenching hunger, wrung him, razed him. At last. *At last.*

He rested his forehead against hers, in her depths, overwhelmed, transported, listening to her delirium, to his. Her graceful back was a deep arch, letting him do it all to her. Blind, out of his mind, he lifted her, filled his savage mouth and hands with her flesh. He had to finish her, leave no fiber of her being uninundated with pleasure. He withdrew all the way out of her then thrust back, fierce and full, riding her wild cry.

It took no more than that. One thrust finished her. And him. Her satin screams echoed his roars as for the first time he jetted his pleasure inside her without barriers. Her convulsions spiked at the first splash of his seed against her womb, their hearts spiraling out of control in a paroxysm of release, one sustained seizure that destroyed the world around them.

Then it was another life, another time where nothing existed except being merged with her, rocking together, riding the aftershocks, still pouring himself into her, feeling her around him, inside and out, sharing the descent. Aliyah. His again.

It had been beyond control, beyond description. Everything. Yet not enough. Would anything ever be?

He realized she'd gone limp in his arms only when she lurched, a gasp seeming to restart her breathing. He withdrew a bit, kept them merged as he looked down at her. She seemed disoriented, her eyes slumberous as they gazed up at him, fathomless. A goddess of temptation and delirium and fulfillment, something every man dreamed of but never really expected to find. His hands dug into her buttocks, gathering her tighter to him.

Her eyes squeezed shut as she gasped again, her core, molten with their combined pleasure, contracting around his still fully engorged erection, making him thrust deeper into her, wrenching moans from both their depths. Her eyes snapped open, scorched him to the bone with the amalgam of pleasure and pain that transfigured her amazing beauty.

He hardened even more, the cataclysm of minutes before serving only to whet his appetite. As it always had. Whenever he'd taken her in a fury of haste, the satisfaction had only shown him what more leisurely mutual pleasuring would bring. And that had been when he'd been far less experienced and ignorant of one paramount fact. That no other woman would do. Ever.

The silence, but for their still-strident breathing, finally registered. The consummation drums had stopped.

His lips twitched. They thought he must have done it already and went about serving dinner, did they?

While it was a reasonable deduction, considering his state when he'd whisked her away, they surely didn't think he'd pounce on an uninitiated virgin in the time frame their drumming lasted? What kind of barbaric king did they think they had? Though he'd probably given the whole world that impression.

But then they'd seen Aliyah. They must think it a wonder he had lasted as long as he had before he'd hauled her off to bed. Not that he cared what anyone thought. He cared only about this. These moments. This woman, this domination, this surrender.

He cared about another thing. Finding a bed. Taking his bride against a door in a frenzy had not been what he'd had in mind. He'd planned to drive her to madness, push her over the brink time and again, until she begged, wept for him. As she'd once done.

But no matter. The night hadn't even started. Though, on a sobering note, if fast and ferocious had been this mind-blowing, they might not survive the night he had in store for them.

His heart boomed. Aliyah, limp again, leaving it up to him to support her, slumped over his chest, humming a sound that thrummed pride and contentment in his chest. He *had* satisfied her, as she had him. Not that he was fully satisfied. Would he ever be?

Minutes later, he could move again. He gathered his armful of satisfied woman more securely and strode through the foreign territory that would become their private playground, which they'd inaugurated at its very entrance with an act of abandon and total pleasure. He would make sure every corner of these extensive apartments received the same treatment.

He walked with her wrapped around him inside and out, her eyes averted, an unfathomable expression coating her heavenly face, glowing with mystery and satisfaction under the hypnotic lights emanating from dozens of polished brass lanterns resting on the floor, hanging on the walls, and from the soaring ceiling.

Incense fumes added to the dreamlike quality of it all, dancing among the beams, around them, like scented ghosts, as he took her through one room to the next, seeking the bedchamber. Then he found it.

He stood at its threshold taking it all in.

Yes. This was what he'd envisioned. What he'd demanded. A chamber fit for pleasuring his queen in.

Beneath the central dome, draped in a bronze bedcover and deep red sheets and gauzy curtains, lay the twelve-foot, four-poster bed in the middle of a forty-foot arabesque hardwood platform raised five steps over the rest of the chamber.

On the left, by the windows overlooking the sea, resting on a mosaic marble floor strewn with acres of Persian silk carpets, was the arrangement of stools to bend her over, the platforms to serve her over and service her on, the couches to ride her or be ridden by her on. On the right by windows designed to let in the sun so they could sunbathe in seclusion, on another platform was the sunken water-jet tub where he would soothe her before taking her back to bed, or taking her there again. On the north end was the one thing he'd always wanted to try. A swing, specially designed for lovemaking. And then there were the mirrors, strategically placed for their optimum viewing pleasure. And he already had new ideas for things he'd have to install. For now, he'd settle for what he had to work with.

Tonight, the first of many to come, would make up for the agony of the first few hours of all the years without her.

He laid her on the bed gently, careful not to disrupt their merging, started to undo the rest of that outfit that had already entered history, that would be featured forever in his wildest fantasies, which he'd bring out again and again to reenact this night. He bent to suckle and nibble every inch of luscious flesh he uncovered, so different yet still her, and groaned, "So, my rule-pulverizing, *joloos*-crashing, black-wearing, sword-wielding *maleekah*…was your deflowering to your satisfaction?"

Another flood of tremors drenched Aliyah's body.

Or they could be aftershocks. Or continuous miniorgasms.

She couldn't believe he had her spiraling again. He was really merciless, must know what he was doing to her. He was teasing her about it, after all, as he remained inside her, bigger, harder rocking into her gently as if to soothe the ferocity with which he'd claimed her, and only managing to compromise her sanity again. As she was sure he meant to do.

Another gush flooded her core at the memory of those cataclysmic moments. She'd plunged into a fugue state from the moment he'd hauled her into his arms, the drums beating in her blood, driving her into a frenzy, turning her body into a vise around him, her tongue into a lash to make him go faster, do it

Then he'd done it, plunged inside her, and it was like her whole being had imploded with the release of seven years' worth of frustration and yearning. She'd never known such acute, explosive pleasure. She'd almost feared it was damaging things inside her.

She'd thought she'd been drained, never to recharge again. Then he'd moved again, and she was back to the starting point the need drilling into her as if it had never been assuaged.

He now played her with those fingers, power and virility made into bronze perfection, like the virtuoso he was, removing her jewelry, rumbling in that bass voice that reverberated where reason and self-preservation never visited. "Seeing you in this outfit, adorned in these…I wanted to take you straight here, strip them off, take you. I don't know how I lasted when I could smell your arousal, feel the same hunger twisting in your gut. You were so ready, you're so ready still, so wet and hot, you scorch me."

She arched as he picked up her feet, brought them to his

shoulders, tickled her legs with his hair-roughened face, undid her high-heeled sandals, left her *kholkhal* on, drove deeper into her until she moaned, "And you're congratulating yourself that I was? Maybe it was the duel that had me so hot and bothered."

He bit into her calf, distant thunder or a bound beast rumbling deep in his chest. "*Ya Ullah*, I can't contest that. It's a testament to my control that I didn't drag you to the ground right there. That was the most erotic foreplay we've ever indulged in, on a totally new level to anything we've ever known. I bet we've entered the annals of history as the king and queen who gave the world a new sexual fantasy."

She gasped as he raised her buttocks off the bed, slit her *lehenga* in two from the zipper down. She clamped his head between her legs as he kneaded her thighs, singed them in moist kisses, abraded them with the rough silk of his facial hair.

She twisted, bucked with every touch, moaned, "You're getting this fixed. I want my historical outfit intact."

"I'm making you a dozen replicas, but this stays shredded. This is still a historical artifact. You get to show it to the coming generations, brag how your king couldn't bear to be outside you long enough to take it off."

He laid her back on the bed, came down on his knees, dragged her hips over his thighs, opened her around his bulk as he started to take off his own clothes. She whimpered as each button, each shrug revealed more, then more to her starving eyes.

She'd been wrong. He hadn't just been upgraded, he'd metamorphosed. This was what the next step of evolution had to look like. And he was being too generous with his assets, as he'd put it, exposing them in that agonizing striptease he'd devised for her, as she lay helpless before him, beneath him, impaled on his potency, inundated with his beauty, his hunger, pleasure echoing inside her, new sparks gathering into another storm.

Then he was naked from the waist up, his pants opened onl
to free his erection. The sight, the way he spread her and cam
prowling over her like a ravenous tiger, his hands seeking he
secrets, her triggers, made her buck again, clamp her arms aroun
his head, her fingers stabbing into the luxury of his raven silk hair
bunching, kneading, needing. He gave, plunged into her gaspin
mouth, the taste she'd craved for years maddening her wit
hunger, all of him even more arousing with the amalgam of hi
upgraded assets, the stamp of maturity and power, the alien fee
of his facial hair.

"Tell me, *ya maleekati*," he groaned into her lips, filling he
lungs with his breath, his scent. "You were always generou
with your confessions, open in your demands. Tell me how muc
I pleasured you, tell me what you want now, Aliyah."

Hearing her name pouring from his lips like that, dark, fath
omless, almost…moved, brought back all the times he'd groane
it to her on rising arousal, roared it from the heights of release
whispered it from the depths of satiation, branding her soul a
surely as he'd branded her body and senses….

But it hadn't been real then. It wasn't real now.

The slash of misery across her heart was surely a moroni
reaction. She already knew that.

She tore her lips away, panted, "You want verbal adulation
Not satisfied with all the practical evidence I gave you that m
body 'wants you with the same ferocity still'?"

His hands paused, one cupping her breast, the other wher
he'd been massaging her where they were joined.

Then he withdrew them. After one hard-breathing momen
he moved, dislodged himself from her depths, his groan echoin
hers at the pain of separation.

He heaved himself up off of her, off the bed, rose to his fe
in one gravity-defying move. It had to be to propel that bulk wi
that effortless economy. With one heavy-lidded look, he turne

climbed down the platform, every motion speaking of inborn grace and control, of extensive discipline and power.

He reached one side of the chamber, where an honest-to-goodness sunken bath the size of a small pool was inbuilt in another platform similar to the one that housed the bed. He pushed a few buttons and started water running, opened vials and splashed generous amounts of their contents into the water. In seconds, the combined scents of musk and jasmine rose over the distinctive, welcome scent of steam in this dry atmosphere.

Then he turned, and she realized she was still spread-eagled in that do-anything-to-me pose. Mortified, furious, she forced some voluntary movement into her molten limbs, tried to assume a position that didn't scream "female in heat."

He stood there, watching her struggling with the incredible hybrid lace/silk/satin blanket she was lying on, trying to cover a portion of her nakedness. When she'd done all she was capable of doing, he walked back to her. The cathedral-size chamber shrank and air disappeared.

He came to stand over her, his eyes flaring and subsiding like a pulsar star as his hands slid down his body, watching her reaction intently as he completed his striptease. She was sure it provided him with total gratification. By the time he was fully exposed, dauntingly engorged, she was back on her back, panting.

But instead of taking the spoils of yet another victory over her, his eyes gentled…*gentled*. His voice, damn him, followed suit. "What went on before today is no more, Aliyah. Why keep bringing up what no longer exists?"

She choked on incredulity. "Whoa. That would be a great argument in a homicide trial. Why bring up the victim who no longer exists? Why bring up the murder since it's in the past? Way to go on that brilliant piece of absolutist, revisionist crap."

His eyes sobered, but his lips spread. "Every single word you say, every breath and look—*you* are an aphrodisiac of such concentration and effect that I could dilute you and dispense you to the world and cure all sexual dysfunction. But though I love to tangle tongues with you in every way, I'm not letting you drag us into a vicious circle of blame and bitterness. Whatever happened in the past, we were different people then."

She gave an indelicate snort. "You were a different man five days ago when you threw that bit of offensive arrogance at me, asserting I still wa—"

He pounced on her, effectively silencing her, snatched her up in his arms as if she weighed nothing and strode to the sunken bath.

He descended into the water with her, maneuvered her so that she ended up straddling him. She moaned long and loud at the sensory overload of feeling hair-roughened, satin-skinned, rock-hard flesh pressing against hers, perfect warmth enveloping her, and the soothing ingredients he'd added to the bath pampering her skin and senses.

Before he made another argument for the necessity of leaving the past in the past, she decided to preempt him, say something. "About the *joloos*-crashing bit…" Her breath caught as he gently untangled the pins dangling from her hair where he'd taken off her *dupatta*, coiled the masses of locks and pinned them up so they wouldn't get wet.

He didn't answer her until he was running patterns of lather all over her arms and breasts and thighs and stomach, until she felt he'd forever burned out all her neural transmissions. "I always forecast everything with almost infallible accuracy. But I didn't see that coming. I didn't think you'd want to see more of me than you absolutely had to."

"Who says I wanted to see you? I wanted to see a *joloos*." Her distressed gasp didn't sound too convincing.

His eyes, heavy with knowing, with arousal, his erection jumping to slap her buttocks like a spanking hand, told her he wasn't buying it, not for a second.

Then as if to answer her dismissal, he gathered her to him, drank her lips dry, then moved to her neck, her arms, her breasts, her hands, each ministration jackknifing stimulation through her, until she wailed, *"Kamal."*

The beast inside him rumbled again. *"Ella, essrokhi essmi haik,* scream my name like that, *ya maleekati.* I'm glad you *joloos*-crashed, *sam'ah?* Do you hear? Deliriously glad."

He dipped her into the water, rinsed her off, swept her around in the fluid silk, swam her to the other end of the tub, lifted her out and spread her on her back on the platform. Then he came over her, exposed her to all forms of sensual exploration, from her toes to her fingertips, from the inside of her thighs to her ears, all the time returning to her mouth to whisper more aroused, arousing words. *"Ya Ullah,* what have you done with yourself? There shouldn't be beauty like this. But there you are. Did you feel, did you *see* what you did to me? Do to me?"

In answer she showed him what *he* did to *her,* writhing beneath him, her hands flailing over whatever she could reach of him. She twisted over him, had his mind-blowing potency where she craved it, in her watering mouth. He let her have him, explore the daunting girth and length with darting tongue and trembling hands, growling his enjoyment of her homage. *"Aih, emlokini*…own me."

She was lapping his arousal off the smoothest silk head, the cramping between her legs clenching on more rushes of molten agony as she wondered how she'd ever been able to accommodate that much demand, when his hands on her shoulders stopped her. She cried out in chagrin and frustration, only to find herself on her back again. She held out her arms, hurrying him, welcoming him, but he only descended on his knees in the whirling water and pulled her legs over his shoulders.

She tried to sit up, panting, "I want you, Kamal, *you*…"

"And you'll have me, every way you want me, but first…"

He nibbled her inner thighs, along the lips enveloping her womanhood, had her thrashing and crying out, needing more, closer, *there,* but he wouldn't give it to her. When he had her almost weeping, he suddenly blew his hot, ragged breath on her knot of nerves. The sound that came from her was alien, hunger made audible. She was mindless now. Nothing left but craving and sensation. The emptiness inside her was spreading, engulfing her.

"You're killing me…so empty…fill me, Kamal, fill me…"

In response he slipped two long, careful fingers inside her.

She screamed. He added a third finger as he kneaded her breasts, pinched her nipples. She thrashed and begged for him some more. He only drove deeper inside her and quakes started radiating from the point where her inner flesh clamped around his fingers, rippling out violently, her every cell hurtling with frightening speed toward an explosive release.

He rubbed his scratchy face feverishly against her tender flesh, like a lion roughly nuzzling his mate, growled, sounded like one. "*Bte'raffi k'm ana ja'aan*…do you know how hungry I am? For your taste? How long I've starved?"

Then he lowered his lips to her core. With his first voracious lick, she collapsed back on herself, becoming one tight pinpoint of insanity. She hovered there for one endless heartbeat. Then he sucked her flesh inside his mouth, drew on it soft then harder, tongued it slow then faster and she exploded. Ceased to exist. Dissipated in wave after tidal wave of white-hot release.

An eternity later, the convulsions racking her body eased and she focused on his regal head between her thighs, where she'd thought she'd never see it again, drawing out her aftermath, draining her of every spark of pleasure her body was capable of.

She closed her eyes on an out-of-body sensation, surrendered to his ministrations until he dried her with huge, white cotton towels, then picked her up and strode with her back to the bed,

He came down half over her, propped himself on his elbow, his other hand and eyes cascading over her with caresses and intentions of what he still had in mind for her, his erection throbbing into her thigh. And just like that, her hunger rose again, had her reaching for him. He stopped her, smiled.

"I can wait now. I'm even reveling in the agony. Before, I think I would have had a stroke if I hadn't taken you. It was a merciful thing that I didn't have to initiate you."

She was really surprised her voice was still working when she smirked, "You must be congratulating yourself for having already done the groundwork seven years ago."

He stiffened, went still. For what felt like ten minutes. Then he finally drawled, "Are you implying that *I* initiated you?"

She stared at him. "That is a euphemism for taking my virginity, right? God, this is just too rich. You didn't *notice?*"

He withdrew the hand that had stilled on her left buttock, sat up, his face frightening with its lack of life and emotion. His voice was as lifeless when he said, "There was no blood."

"And that is what also went missing from the scene today, huh? You no doubt would have loved to dip another pristine royal handkerchief into the proof of my innocence to wave it to joyous Judarians from the ramparts."

"This is a huge claim you're making."

She gaped at the gleam of anger, of danger in his eyes.

It made her reckless. "It's not a claim," she spat. "It's the truth. I thought you knew, that it was obvious."

His vision seemed to turn inward, as if he were replaying memories, watching them more closely this time. "There was a tinge of blood, but I thought it was because I was too big for you. You *were* as tight as a virgin…"

"And how many virgins have you 'deflowered'? Or since the criterion here is tightness, 'untightened'?"

"Since you're as tight as you ever were, I evidently haven't 'untightened' you. But in answer to your question, none. Not counting you, as you claim. I never accept offers from women who aren't my equals in sexual experience."

"Do any exist, who don't charge by the hour?" He narrowed his eyes. She hurtled on. "And how do you know they're your equal? Do their bids to share your bed come with detailed résumés? Deflowered in the class of 1998, obtained a master's in fellatio in 2000 and a Ph.D. in indiscriminate sex in 2004? Do their applications come with long lists of referrals and recommendations?"

He bit his lip. Then he shook his head and barked a rough laugh. "That would be a valuable tool in selecting bed partners, thank you for the recommendation." His lips spread on a lethal smile as anger still simmered in his eyes, felt more at himself now for succumbing to her bitter humor. "But so far I haven't needed more than a woman's attitude and reputation to categorize her. Neither of yours were that of a virgin."

She closed her eyes. She wanted this conversation to be over. Erased. What had gotten into her to bring it up at all?

But how could she have guessed he hadn't known? It had been one more reason to abhor him, thinking he'd used her so badly.

She turned her head away. "Listen, it doesn't matter."

He brought her face back to his, the gentleness in his touch surprising her so much she opened her eyes, drowned in the honeyed depths of his as he whispered, "You think you can drop something like this on me, then try to dismiss it?"

"So what do you want me to do? Apologize? I do. I am beyond sorry that I was so stupid I fell in your bed that fast. But then that comes with the territory of being too inexperienced to live."

His eyes lost all expression. Then he finally drawled, "You're experienced now."

"And how." He'd once made her experience things she hadn't even heard about. Looking around this fable-setting of a chamber that had been revamped for a "king in his prime," she was sure he'd broaden her experience to new "swinging" heights.

After another silence, he murmured, "Did I hurt you?"

Hurt her? He hurt her by just existing, just breathing.

At her silence he persisted. "I know you had an orgasm when I took you. It was so powerful the pleasure of it almost blew my head apart with the power of my own release. But I was rough, and it doesn't matter that it was beyond me to stop, or that you responded so fiercely that you shredded whatever flimsy tatters of control I had left. Are you in any pain or discomfort now?"

After all the pampering and pleasuring he'd just drowned her in? Or was that just a mandatory question before he gave her an even rougher ride? She quirked an eyebrow. "What if I said yes?"

His lips crooked as he ran a forefinger between her breasts down to her belly button, then downward, stopping only an inch from where the throb of demand for him was becoming a pounding. "I'd soothe you, heal you, make you come until you faint."

Again? Out loud she said, "You mean you won't...uh...?"

He followed his fingers with his lips and tongue and teeth, rumbling into her. "Thrust inside you? Fill you? Ride you? Pound you into the bed, ram you against the wall, have you rise and fall on me on that swing until you're bucking and screaming in an agony of release beneath me, against me, around me?" He raised his eyes from where his fingers tormented one breast, gave her nipple another graze that had her bucking off the bed "No. I won't. You'll have to beg me to."

And she decided to leap without looking again. Her crash was predestined, why guard against it? "Okay. I beg you."

"W'Ullah ma beyseer, it doesn't work that way. This is the part where I make you pass out from too much pleasure."

"I did pass out against that door. So your objective has already been fulfilled. How about we move on to the next stage?"

He rose above her, throwing his head back on a sound between a growl and a laugh. "You would tempt *ash-shaytaan*."

"I *am* tempting a devil." She lunged for him, her teeth and fingers sinking into solid, polished power-made-man, her senses drowning in an overdose of virility.

He laughed again, lunged back at her, drowned her in a luxurious, tongue-mating embrace. When her moans became incessant he suddenly started extricating himself from her clinging limbs. She whimpered, tried to drag him back, but he restrained her hands. "Patience. This time, I'm doing this right."

She tried to drag him back with her legs. "You did it right the first time. Just do it again."

He bent and bit into one of the thighs clinging to him. "I will do it, again and again. But I have to do something first."

He freed himself, got off the bed, strode toward the arches ringing the space, disappeared behind one of the Arabian-style columns. What was that tormentor doing? Playing hide-and-seek?

Just as she was about to go seek him, the lights of all the lanterns dimmed then went out, plunging the chamber in total darkness, since the windows were covered in layers of drapery.

She lay there in the dark, her heart thudding. What did he have in mind? They'd never made love in the dark, what with there being so much to see. He had once blindfolded her, though, and she'd gone wild. Well, wilder than usual. Was this what he was…?

Suddenly a loud, droning sound, like a metal monster moaning made her jump.

Just before she sprang off the bed and went for him, a slash of silver light fell on the bed. She gaped as it widened like a huge opening eye, until it had engulfed the whole bed, like a celestial spotlight. It took her many stunned heartbeats to raise her eyes and find out that that was a very apt description.

The dome—the whole, dang hundred-foot ceiling dome—had

folded on both sides to leave the chamber open to the night sky. And the full moon was almost right over the bed.

"This is how you should be showcased…" She jumped again at Kamal's bass rasp as he seemed to materialize before her moonstruck eyes, a colossal shadow detaching from the darkness that had spawned him. "A goddess of sensual abandon and wanton desires, of rampant pleasures, waiting for worshippers to come pay homage, glowing, ripe, voracious, spellbinding."

She was all that? Not that she was about to contradict him. She'd let him say whatever he wished. As long as it was no longer abuse.

He came into the circle of light, the perpendicular illumination casting harsh shadows over the hewn sculpture of his face, turning it from regal to supernatural, his body from incredible to overwhelming. His hair glowed with Prussian highlights as he pushed her back on the bed, loomed over her, the full moon blazing at his back, turning him into a heart-pounding silhouette, only his eyes catching its silver beams, glowing like embers. She went limp beneath him with the power of it all, the sheer brutal beauty, her broken heart splintering in her chest with the violent hope that it meant something—that *she* meant something for him to give her all this.

Her chest tightened on the jagged pieces. She cried out with the pain. Her desperation released some shackle that had been holding him back and he pressed between her eagerly spreading thighs. He let her feel his dominance for a fraught moment. Then holding her eyes, he growled, *"Aliyah…"* and plunged inside her in one long thrust.

Her body jerked in profound sensual shock. At seeing the pleasure of possessing her seizing his face. At the power of the hot, vital glide of his thick, rigid shaft in her core.

Her legs clamped around him high over his back, giving him fuller surrender. He ground deeper into her until his whole length was buried inside her, filling her beyond capacity. Sensation sharpened, shredding her. She cried out again, tears flowing now.

He started moving inside her, letting go of her eyes only to run fevered appreciation over her body, watching her every quake and grimace of pleasure, growling driven, tormenting things. "There shouldn't be wanting like this...*pleasure* like this...*hat'janenini*..."

She keened and he devoured the explicit sound, his tongue invading her mouth, mimicking his body's movements inside her.

It was he who drove her crazy. What he said, what he was, the friction and fullness of his flesh in hers, the fusion, knowing it was all she had of him, that it would end...

She cried out her desolation and his plunges grew longer, as did her cries until they merged, until she clawed at him, begged. Only then did he ride her harder, building to the jarring rhythm that would finish her, his eyes burning coals, his face taut with savage need, sublime in beauty in the blazing moonlight. She fought back ecstasy, greedy for the moment his seized him.

He realized, growled, "Come for me, *ya maleekati,* let me see what I do to you."

She thrashed her head. "Come with me..."

He roared something scalding and thrust deeper, destroyed her restraint. Release buffeted her with the force of a bursting dam, razed her body in convulsions. Those peaked to agony when he succumbed to her demand, gave her what she craved. Him, at the mercy of the ecstasy she gave him, pleasure racking him, his seed filling her in hard jets. She felt it all, and shattered.

Time and space vanished as he melted into her, grounded the magic into reality, eased her back into her body.

Everything came back into jarring focus when he tried to move off her. She caught him. His weight should have been crushing, but was only anchoring, necessary...

He rose on outstretched arms, his silhouette thudding in her heart, his eyes gleaming satisfaction over her ravished state. He trailed a gently abrasive hand over her, drawled, harsh and sexy, "And tomorrow, *ya maleekati,* we make love under the sun."

The images pierced her vitals as he drowned her in abandon again. Lost, she dragged him right back into delirium.

She was too weak. She was giving him all of her, again. After he'd made it clear he abhorred marrying her, despised nothing more than her. Now he'd despise her more. Her only recourse was to treat this as nothing more than sex. Maybe then she'd be spared the degradation of his knowing she'd never stopped loving him.

For now, she gave it all to him. In the morning, and every minute from then on, she would have to retrieve enough of herself to survive when it was over.

If there was anything left to retrieve.

Eight

Kamal woke up in heaven.

And it was no illusion brought on by opening his eyes to the dawn sky. It was the reality of the goddess draped over him like a sated cover.

This had to be heaven. What he'd thought he'd never have again, the unity with the one person who'd ever matched him on every vital level. But no. This time, what they'd shared had so outstripped the past, he had no word for it but heaven.

Wasn't heaven supposed to be more than one could dream of, full of pleasure for the senses and the mind and the spirit, brimming with exhilaration and energy and an infinity of possibilities, never predictable, always delightful, intriguing, awe-inspiring? Not to mention fulfilling in every way conceivable yet leaving one perpetually hungry for more, ready for anything and willing to go any distance for it?

If so, then heaven was what he'd shared with Aliyah, everything she'd given him, of the fullness of her being.

The heart that raced only from severe exertion boomed now, with the memories, with the expectation of accumulating more. With the feel of her, cleaved to that heart as if she were a vital organ that he'd been living without, that had been restored to him.

His heart kicked into a higher gear. She was stirring.

He breathed in relief, freed at last from the fear of interrupting her much-needed slumber, let his stinging hands luxuriate in cascading down her firm velvet skin.

She went still again, until he thought she'd gone back to sleep. But her heart was beating so hard he could feel its frantic rhythm slap against his own chest, reverberate inside it, mingling their heartbeats, sending his haywire.

No, she was awake. And remembering. Reliving. And her body was readying itself for more. He felt the coolness of sleep evaporating on a blast of heat that radiated from her core. And he couldn't wait, for more of her, her wit and vitality and unpredictability and hunger. *Ya Ullah,* her hunger. Besides everything about her, it was that that sent the beast inside him howling, recognition of the only mate made to want him, fully, no-holds-barred. Her breath was hitching now and he lost his battle with impatience.

He tightened his arms, one around her back, the other over her hips, grinding her into the hardness that hadn't subsided since he'd laid eyes on her again.

She surrendered to his embrace for a moment, then pushed against him, raised herself on her arms, looked down at him, her eyes in shadow, her magnificent waterfall of hair gleaming with copper overtones in the strengthening daylight.

"I can see, uh, make that *feel,* that you're ready for round six," she quipped. "Or is it seven? I guess it is, since there was this time you finally let me wave your other…sword."

He went still, her words hitting him like a dark, cold flood.

Last night, after that second time he'd made love to her, she'd lavished words of passion and craving on him, hot and fervent portrayals of what he made her feel, candid and beautiful and laden with emotion. And when he'd let her have her desire, owning him, suckling and fondling and doing whatever she pleased to bring him to an explosive completion in her eager mouth, she'd turned the experience into something sublime in intensity, in meaning.

She sounded anything but sublime now. Almost…slutty, for real this time.

He moved, needing to put some distance between them to deal with the slap of disappointment, the drain of euphoria.

She flipped onto her back on the bed, sighed. "So not ready, after all, huh? That's just the way you wake up, huh? I wouldn't know since I never woke up with you. My bad."

Every word, every inflection grated on suddenly raw nerves.

How fast, how completely she could plunge him from heaven to vile reality. Only she had ever done anything like that to him.

But…he could be overreacting. Could be misinterpreting her words. She could just be groping for levity, not knowing what to say to him after the transfiguring night they'd shared. Maybe the past was still blocking her ability, outside moments of extreme passion, to deal with him in a normal, unaffected manner. Maybe she didn't know what last night meant, where he wanted to go from here and was securing herself a face-saving way back to the old hostility, in case that was where he ended up taking them.

All his rationalizations crashed and burned when she went on, "Not that I'm criticizing or anything. Boy, have you got stamina. Last night was definitely the best sex I've had in forever."

Disappointment exploded inside him. Unable to curb it anymore, he turned to her. But she'd gotten out of bed, was breezing by him, heading to the bath chamber.

He struggled with the need to storm after her, shake her, demand that she explain herself. Had nothing changed? Had she not? Last night, her claim that he'd been her first had shaken him with the implications. If it had been true, how had she found it so easy to leave his arms and fall into those of others? Had he whetted her appetite and she'd decided to sample the variety of lovers on offer? Then another implication had forced itself into being. That maybe he'd misconstrued the whole situation, condemned her based on false reports and circumstantial evidence.

But her attitude now said he'd been a damned fool to even consider this. She herself had admitted she'd become very experienced after his alleged "untightening" of her.

So what did it all mean? The past and the present remained the same? She'd been then and remained now a faithless woman incapable of feeling anything of real depth beyond her insatiable desires? Where did that leave them? Leave him? Where he'd been six days ago, with anger and bitterness and disillusion forever preying on him? How could he go back, now that he knew how much more he could have had, they could have had, if she hadn't been crippled in this devastating, irredeemable way?

The faint sounds of a shower running interrupted his rising turmoil with unwilling images of her with water sluicing down her lushness. He tried to banish them, stop their invasion, stem his yearning for what he could never have.

But they were only joined by more fantasies and memories that overwhelmed his reason, put out the fresh flames of disillusion and disappointment. And he succumbed.

This was far stronger than he was. What they shared, without any higher meaning or emotion, should be enough. It was far more than most marriages had. Royal marriages especially. So what if it was all wrapped around an illusion? What if physical ecstasy was all they could share? He could only wallow in it. For now.

Slow, determined steps took him inside the bath chamber. He stopped at the threshold and watched her, two dozen feet away, in the large shower cubicle, standing there, inert, letting the steady stream of hot water pummel her.

In a minute he was entering the cubicle, advancing on her.

She raised fragile eyes to him and his heart quivered. Was she…? Before hope even formed, her eyes slid down his body, her lips caught in her teeth. Then she melted against the marble wall and drawled, "This time, I bet you're ready."

His heart turned stone-cold steady as hope ebbed away and he plastered himself over her, grabbed her thighs, letting a measured roughness enter his touch as he hauled her up, sliding her against the wall, opening her over his hips.

"Two things you need to know. I'm always ready." He thrust up into her tight warmth, his groan of acute pleasure and heartache echoing her sharp cry. He rested inside her, wishing, regretting, hating the words he had to say to echo hers. Then he said them. "And you're the best sex I've had in…a while."

Kamal took a step back. Then two more. Then he paused.

Transfixing. Disturbing. A chaos of depths and sufferings and insights so sharp it cut, deep and deadly. As for the talent, that was almost painful to behold, to experience.

He moved closer again, hesitant, as if afraid that on closer exposure the painting would damage his psyche. And that might not be too far-fetched a notion. He did feel pain so intense, despondency so inescapable, just looking at it.

What must have Aliyah been feeling when she'd painted it?

This was the last painting. His collection was now complete. He now owned every painting she'd ever created. He kept them to himself in a chamber no one entered but him, to pore over, in his endeavors to fathom the mind of the woman who was his lover and wife and queen, maybe one day to reach it, and her heart.

He'd made many people's fortunes in the last six weeks, those discerning enough to have bought her work. The moment any of them had gotten wind of who was buying, they'd made a grab at an impossible price. He hadn't even thought it worth a second's hesitation, to haggle, or to use leverage to force them to accept a reasonable price. He'd even wanted them to have whatever they asked for. For what price was too high, was even fitting, to place on Aliyah's talent and suffering?

And there was no doubt in his mind. All the works she'd painted since she'd relinquished her modeling career years ago, that had been carving her a place among the modern masters, were a manifestation, a gloomy, oppressive almost tangible depiction of inner turmoil so great, so warping, he was even more awed by her current stabilization, her bone-deep steadiness and change.

Yes. Change. For the absolute best. He'd felt it in his heart, and every minute he spent with her brought more and more proof. He'd become certain her words that morning after had been a self-protecting maneuver. He'd known it even as he'd tried to take her in cold-blood and had ended up losing himself in the conflagration of their passion.

He'd since surrendered to their soaring intimacy and rapport, to his delight in discovering her as she was now.

One thing remained. The key to her transformation.

He'd spent the years battling the need to know everything about her. But since their first married day, he'd been indulging in researching every detail of her past seven years.

He'd found little information about her. It was as if she'd ceased to exist after he'd left her. It was so confusing, he wondered where the rumors that had run rampant had originated from, could only rationalize they'd just been echoes of her life before he'd met her. He'd found no evidence to guide him except her paintings. And they'd been a gutting shock. The first time he'd laid eyes on one, he'd almost wept. Such pain, such instability, such desperation, such a struggle to contain it all.

He could only think this had been exactly how she'd contained it all, purged it. And it *had* been purged. Now—when she wasn't acting as his queen, her unique combination of wit and wisdom, tolerance and fire making her a perfect foil for him, making her a consort he couldn't have dreamed of—she painted. And the difference in her work was astounding. As addiction and volatility had once soiled her psyche and bled their desperation onto the canvas, now stability and serenity colored her huge range. Her sensitivity, her insight, her genius—they had him spellbound.

His phone beeped. Aliyah. He'd set his alarm for her daily painting session. He was getting addicted to watching her.

He placed his acquisition with its counterparts, locked the walk-in cabinet then strode out of the chamber.

In minutes he was entering Aliyah's northern-lit atelier, found her already at her easel, wearing that stained-beyond-redemption painting coat that she adamantly refused to part with, that she told him he should be thankful she even washed.

His blood ran thick and hot at the mere sight of her, his flesh hardening, his heart melting. Then he noticed the way she was undulating in her chair and realized. She was listening to her iPod, which was no doubt blaring Mozart.

Feeling free to come closer, to watch her longer without her noticing, he came into the room as she prepared her gear. Then she took the cover off her work in progress, and his heart stopped.

Him. She was painting him. And not from a photo. From memory. He well knew. He'd surely never taken a photo like that. He'd never *seen* anything like that. Not from this end.

In the painting that was almost finished, he was leaning at an angle that made it clear he was on top of someone—her—his every muscle bunched and gleaming with the full moon blazing in the night sky at his back, his face and eyes burning with an inextricable amalgam of ferocious emotions.

His heart filled again, stampeded, his eyes stung, his every cell hurt. No one—*no one* had ever done anything like that for him. There *was* nothing like that. The thought, the time, the effort, the depiction of everything he'd felt, the virtuosity of its translation into a likeness that was almost supernatural in accuracy. It was as if she'd absorbed his essence and that of those magical moments into her being and then poured them onto the canvas, with her talent as the conduit. That she had seen and understood all he'd felt, that she'd been so moved she'd needed to bring this miracle into existence. A portrait of his soul.

Aliyah, everything she did… *Too much.*

At the last moment he stopped himself from hurtling to her, grabbing her, smothering her in kisses, mingling her with his being, just so he could breathe again after she'd taken his breath away. Instead he forced himself to walk back out. She might not want to share this with him now. Or at all. He shouldn't intrude on her. But he needed—he needed *her.* He just had to touch her, be close to her. *Now, Aliyah,* now.

"Kamal?"

He sent up a prayer of thanks. She'd felt him, called him.

He reopened the door a crack. "May I come in?"

She scrunched her face at him. "*Galalet El Mallek* Kamal Aal Masood asking permission to enter a room in his palace? Quick, raise a global alert. Earth is tilting sideways in ten minutes."

She pulled the covers over the painting as she spoke. So she didn't want him to see it. She'd been open with her previous work. Maybe she wanted this to be a surprise. Yes, that was it.

He prowled into the room, deliberately infusing his steps with a calmness that had to be his best act ever. "Save the global alert for when you say I can't enter and I abide by your ban."

She turned to him, radiant with indulgence and teasing. "I didn't say you *can* enter."

He reached her, his hands burning now, his nerves, needing to haul her to him, squeeze her, assimilate her. "I'm in. Want to kick me out? We can have a brush fight."

She looked him up and down, made him feel superhuman, craved to his last spark of being, then she grabbed his jacket's collar, dragged him by it. He fought so he wouldn't pounce on her, let her set the pace. "I do want to propose some heavy brush-work. With some edible colors, all over your edible self."

He shrugged off his jacket, started unbuttoning his shirt. "My body is your canvas, *ya maleekati*. Paint me, devour me."

She jumped off her stool, hugged him hard. "I'll take these as more decrees, *somo'wak,* ones I can't wait to obey. But though there's nothing more I want than to go all impression-ist on you then lick your majesty clean, I have five minutes left of privacy. I need at least five hours for the masterpiece I'll make of you."

He raised her face to his, his breathing constricting with emotion. "I can make five minutes feel like five hours." Then he took her lips, the need too ferocious to tame into preliminaries. Not that he needed any. She met him halfway, on fire, wrench-ing back at him in hot, moist, blind kisses that detonated desire inside him like depth mines as her clothes started dissolving under his ardor. "Five minutes will do…"

"Oh, God, oh, sorry…"

The choking apology hit Kamal between the shoulder blades. He hadn't had five minutes. They were early. Damn them.

He barely unfused his lips from Aliyah's. Then, still unable to take his hands off her, the one beneath her coat pressing her to his erection, the other cupping her breasts, he forced a gruff greeting. "Anna, Farah, *sabah'el khair.*"

"*Sabah'el khair,* King Kamal." The flaming-faced Anna stumbled into a curtsy even though he'd made it clear that, as his mother-in-law, too, she was to call him Kamal and that *he* would kiss her hand, or bow on meeting. He was in no condition to do either now.

Aliyah chuckled breathlessly. "You just made a regal enemy."

Kamal turned his eyes to her, the heat fusing his guts un-quenchable. "A temporary one, most definitely."

"We're going!" Farah chirped, no doubt unable to wait to tell Shehab of another episode in his obdurate brother's vanquishing.

"Stay," he rapped out as he finally untangled their bodies. "I was just passing by before a state meeting."

Aliyah cocked her head as she put her clothes in order, tendrils from her improvised chignon caressing her flushed cheeks. "Sure you won't cause an international incident right now?"

He gazed into her laughing eyes, the eyes he now lived to feel on him, then bent, dropped a word in her ear. *"Labwa."*

And she was, a lioness. Fierce and fearless and free, wanton and totally open about it, letting him revel in it in every second. She now corroborated his aroused hiss, made a growling/purring sound deep in her throat, for his ears only.

Before he dragged her out of there and to hell with her family, he ground her lips in one last hard kiss, turned, took his leave of the ladies and walked out. Aliyah's mind-messing chuckles rang in his ears, then in his mind until he entered his stateroom.

The first thing he did was to postpone his meeting. He needed an hour alone. Maybe his body and mind would subside meanwhile.

He strode to the windows overlooking the sea, saw her face filling its endlessness and that of the sky's. Aliyah.

He could think of nothing but her. Every moment he found new things to appreciate, to bind him to her.

Though he resented her family right this second, at least Anna and Farah, they were just another area where her magnificence had manifested. He still marveled at the way she'd smoothed over the upheavals in her family dynamics, the magnanimity, protectiveness and open-mindedness she'd offered Farah and Anna, the flexible, blame-free, unconditional love she'd extended to her adoptive mother and father and King Atef. All that and everything she did made his admiration all-encompassing, his love absolute.

Yes, love. He could no longer evade his feelings or give them another name. Still, love didn't do what he felt for her justice.

He had loved her in the past, and it had been nothing compared to what he felt now. The woman she'd become hadn't only triumphed over her addiction but had gone in the opposite direction, harnessing her energy into talent and power, becoming a great artist and queen. And she inspired more than love in him. *Eshg. Walah.*

Yes, those came close to describing what he felt for her. Emotion, involvement, commitment, so pure and pervasive they integrated into his being, changed him permanently, unshakable and earth-shaking, worshipful and lustful, asking for no more proof, applying no safeguards, seeing the truth once and forever and laying down everything that he was to enrich her life.

But the blissful present didn't erase the shame of the past.

The more he thought about how long and hard she must have struggled, how he'd had no faith in her, hadn't only left her alone in her struggles but attempted to destroy her before he did, the deeper his distress became.

Worse still, he suspected his crimes were even more serious, that he'd punished her for a nonexistent one. He now believed she couldn't have been unfaithful, let alone promiscuous, not even under the influence of her former addiction. There had to have been another explanation for what she'd done, what he'd seen.

He swung around, buzzed for his helicopter. He was doing this now. He was routing out the scum who'd poisoned him against her.

He would make Shane supply him with that explanation. And then he'd make him pay.

The flight had been long, and his temper had sharpened with every passing second.

But he'd had to come himself, couldn't have brought Aliyah's cousin Shane to Judar. He had to do this away from her, clear up this mess without the least risk of her finding out. He couldn't contemplate having it taint her sensibilities.

So he'd come to Vegas. Not that he was leaving his jet. Shane would be brought to him in—he consulted his watch—two minutes.

He was counting down the seconds, adding another sin to Shane's record with each when *kabeer el yaweran* walked in with a bum in tow. This was him?

Kamal's revulsion rose as he gauged how vice had metamorphosed the fresh-faced twenty-seven-year-old into a balding, potbellied wreck who looked twice his age.

"So we meet again, Kamal." *Kabeer el yaweran* nudged him, and Shane only snorted. "Oh, yes, you're the king of some backward, oil-dripping autocracy now." He gave a mocking deep bow, followed by an obscene finger gesture.

Kamal exhaled, dismissed his men. He wanted no one around as he tore this man apart and got the truth out of his fetid soul.

"Whatever I am, Shane, I'm not an alcoholic and a gambler who's better off dead, according to his own mother."

"She's a hag of a bitch who would drive Satan to drink." Shane leered at him. He'd clearly hit the bottle first thing in the morning. "But you're not here to talk about my literal old woman but about yours. Luscious, mind-destroying Aliyah."

Kamal rose to his feet. "One more disrespectful reference, and I start breaking your flimsy bones. You've been warned."

"Ooh, the big brute defending his beloved's honor. Oh, wait. She's only your winning card in a gamble to hold on to your throne. Ironic, when you once threw her aside like a used tissue."

Too bad Kamal couldn't consider that disrespect to Aliyah. Shane was only recounting incidents that had happened, no matter the reason behind them. He ground out, "I vividly recall your part in that, Shane. Now I want the truth."

"You want the truth, huh? You have a kingdom to play with, billions to squander, the most gorgeous woman alive to exploit, but you want more. What do you want to know, my liege? How I loved Aliyah so much I couldn't breathe sometimes? How I wished you dead since the moment she saw you and forgot that anything else existed? How jealousy ate at me until there was nothing left? Nah. I bet you want me to start at the part when you became aware of my existence."

Kamal's blood tumbled into a boiling fury that he couldn't beat this man speechless. He shredded the words. "Yes, that is what I want."

Shane's bloodshot eyes poured hatred and spite over him. "You know what I thought the moment I opened that door and found you there? That this was my chance to expose you for the depraved son of a bitch I knew you were, before you sucked her dry then spat her out. So I told you what you wanted to hear."

The detonation of rage made Kamal envision himself battering the other man to death. His voice sounded inhuman to his own ears when he hissed, "I wanted to hear that my lover was promiscuous?"

"Promiscuous? How quaint. And you were what, monogamous?"

"I certainly was."

"That's so honorable, dude. You were so committed to her you distrusted her based on an openly spiteful stranger's word. Yeah, I saw you waiting in your car, to check out my story. So I called her, told her I'd fainted but 911 told me to go to E.R. myself. She hurried back, the lovely girl. And you drew your own conclusions, didn't you? You bought my lies and the circumstantial evidence I provided because they gave you the excuse you needed to walk out on her. Sure, you still wanted her, but you thought she wasn't worth the headache of family grumbles and business trouble. You were searching for a clean break where you maintained the moral high ground so you wouldn't feel guilty about dumping the lover who worshipped you. You had to convince yourself that she didn't, that she was worthless. And once you did, you crushed her into the ground.

"Then you found out you needed her, were forced to give her your name, and you're anxious to hear the truth at last. But it's just to make sure that she isn't unworthy of your majesty."

Kamal had gone numb long before Shane finished his tirade. He didn't know what would happen once the numbness wore off, or if he could hear more. But he had to know.

"Were—were you there after I left her?" Kamal rasped.

"You want to know what it did to her when you cut her off, let her humiliate herself over your brutal treatment? It destroyed her. Every day. I hated you when I saw her spirit dying. I hated her because she let you do that to her, wouldn't let me or anyone or anything heal her. And I hated myself when, instead of freeing her of you sooner rather than later, I set off two agonizing years when I feared she'd end up dead."

Kamal swung away, staggered. He couldn't stand any more of the odious man's revelations.

He slumped down in his chair, suffocating. He had to…had to…

He could do nothing under that malevolent, penetrating stare. His hand landed on his armrest. *Kabeer el yaweran* came running.

Kamal barely articulated the words. "Escort Mr. Morgan out."

Shane was taken away, roaring obscenities that Kamal suddenly could no longer hear. The outside world fell away as he hurtled down an abyss of suspicions that had the macabre feel of admissions, that gave Shane's words the texture of truth.

Demons of doubt shrieked at him, slashing him apart with their verdict. Discarding Aliyah might have cut out his heart, but it had eased many problems that had been affecting his image, his credibility. It had certainly taken care of his dread of being involved with another addict. That had been why he'd turned on her so readily, discarded her without a hearing, chosen to believe the circumstantial evidence. He'd taken the easy way out to serve ends he'd valued far above her, to heed his phobias and weaknesses.

If any measure of that was true, when all he'd said and done to her had been undeserved, if he'd caused all the anguish and desperation that had gutted him in her paintings, if he'd done it for those self-preserving reasons, then he deserved a slow death.

He heard his butchered groans through wavering awareness. They brought him back to focus with a blast of self-rage.

He dared suffer? He'd long forfeited that right, that luxury. The only thing he was allowed to do now was make amends, for the rest of his life. The one worthy thing he could do with said life was to restore her, prostrate himself for her forgiveness, her punishment.

But what if either led to the end? What if he opened Pandora's box, and she rejected him and his atonement?

She'd been going up in flames in his arms each time he touched her, was incredible to him in every other way, as she was with everyone. But what if that was just a mixture of succumbing to duty and their sexual magic? What if she was only taking all the pleasure, in an out of bed, that she could in the situation, but was impatient for the day that she was rid of him?

She *had* implied it was all about sex between them after their wedding night. She hadn't repeated that implication, and he'd believed it had been a defense mechanism, but she hadn't even hinted that she loved him again.

No. That wasn't true. She hadn't done so in words, but there'd been endless details that spoke of…of…what? What if he was interpreting emotional depths and loving meanings behind every word and glance and action because he was desperate to? He'd always thought she'd never loved him. But now he believed— knew—she had. What if he'd managed to kill her love forever?

His head fell into his hands. What could he do? Whichever path he treaded, he could end up causing more damage.

If he admitted his crimes, begged forgiveness, he might pulverize their blissful status quo by dredging up her agony. What if he proclaimed his emotions and learned she'd only decided to settle for a loveless marriage, was horrified by his declarations and put an end to it? What if a beneficial deal to all concerned was acceptable to her, but a love match with her former tormentor wasn't?

But if he kept silent, he'd be shortchanging her, depriving her of exacting her rightful retribution and might end up losing her anyway, when she considered her part in their deal done.

Any step in any direction was potentially catastrophic.

He could see only one solution. One that involved no words.

He wasn't one for those, anyway, wouldn't know how to use them to express the depth and magnitude of his love and his regret.

But he was a man of action.

He would *show* her. He would do whatever it took to restore her faith in him, in herself, her pride and self-worth, her love. He'd dedicate his life to that end, and he'd spend that life being hers.

Forever.

Nine

Aliyah stared at the strip in her trembling hand. A line was forming. The moment it became a distinct pink, her legs buckled.

Pregnant.

She leaned her head against the foot of their bed, moaned.

Her hand shook over her flat abdomen, a hail of emotions bombarding her, suffocating her.

She was going to lose Kamal again. This time forever.

But wait...*wait.* Maybe she wouldn't. Maybe things had changed. They *had*. Since their wedding night, after that horrible morning after, when she'd groped for the shield of sexual nonchalance and he'd smacked her back with far worse, things had changed. Right there in that shower.

It had been as if he'd forgotten what he'd said, what had happened in the past. As if he were a new man, far more incredible than his old passionate self before the nightmarish end seven years ago. And what she'd thought had been an unrepeatable experience, that earth-shattering wedding night, had turned into the norm of their lives together, a pattern of escalating and all-encompassing intimacy.

He included her in his duties, sought her counsel, relied on her insights and opinions, gave her every power to act as his queen. He seemed delighted with everything she said and did, doing what only he could do to accommodate her projects and causes, encouraging her to reach for the stars and making it possible for her to soar in every way. And she'd been soaring higher every day.

He, too, seemed constantly high. He concluded most of his duties on site so he'd be near her, had structured his days to ensure leisurely chunks of time together, time that always included them branding each other with pleasure. She'd never seen him so relaxed, so elated, so vital, so heartbreakingly beautiful.

She'd no longer been able to think beyond being with him in the perfection that mirrored his name. It no longer mattered why he'd changed, she'd just grabbed each moment with both hands, drained it of all it afforded her of him and of happiness.

But that was her. She'd chosen to forget all about his deal and the limitations he'd imposed on their relationship. She'd been telling herself that everything he said and did meant he'd changed his mind, no longer wanted this to end. But she could be wrong.

He could only be making the best of the situation, of this marriage, until he achieved his objective. Now he had.

She moaned, pressed her misery into the soaked bedcover.

She had to stop, think. She had to remember the past six indescribable weeks. He couldn't wish this to end. If these past weeks hadn't been about him showing her by actions louder than anything that he was no longer the man who'd mistreated her, that he wanted their marriage to continue, what did they mean? And now that she was carrying his baby, he…he…

Suddenly everything was swept away like fallen leaves in

a storm. She stared down at her body. And with that imagination that could conjure anything, she saw it all. Her flatness swelling day after day as the baby she'd made with Kamal grew healthy and strong inside her. An ecstatic Kamal in raptures of anticipation. A vital, robust baby who shared his beauty and uniqueness...

She moaned again, long and loud, joy shuddering through her.

She knew the joy would be short-lived so she let it take her over, surrendered to jubilation.

It was only minutes later when she paid the price for soaring with a violent crash back to reality.

Reality said Kamal hadn't retracted his deal, his terms. It said this meant that all she'd been reading into his every word and action could only be what she desperately wished for. It said that he could be enjoying their relationship, her abandon, but still had no intention of permanence. It said now that he'd fulfilled his objective, he'd stop making love to her, would become a hostile stranger again until she gave birth and he divorced her...

Noises in the antechamber interrupted her chaotic thoughts, sent her running to the bathroom. *Kamal.* He'd returned from his trip.

She locked the door, wrapped the pregnancy test strip in tissue and threw it in the bin. She splashed her face with water and tried to coax order into her hair, something other than a frenzied expression onto her face and a decision out of the chaos.

She had to tell him. She had to know what he intended, now.

Feeling she'd just decided to jump off a cliff, she walked out. He was standing by the swing, running a finger up and down its silken ropes. Lost under what looked like the weight of the world. Oh, God, how she loved him.

Then he looked up and her heart stumbled then stopped.

The darkness in his face, the urgency, the *enormity* in his eyes...what did they mean? God...was this it? He'd tell her that nothing had changed, that their deal was still on, that he'd been putting up with it all, that she'd been alone in experiencing all the magnificence, was deluded and self-deluding?

It was the hesitation on his face, which she'd never thought to ever see, that broke her. *She couldn't let him say it.*

She flew to him, threw herself at him. He caught her with a groan that seemed to tear up things inside him.

He crushed her in his arms as he sagged onto the swing, took her straddling his hips as she fought to press her lips all over his face, her hands beneath his clothes, to feel him, to free him, to take what she could of him, while she still could.

"Aliyah…" he groaned again as he stopped her before she lowered herself on him, claimed him.

Her lips devoured the rest to keep it unsaid, sobbed her plea into his mouth. "Don't say anything, just let me have this…"

He grunted something driven that lodged into her heart as he bit into her lips, thrust up inside her, over and over again, the swinging motion escalating the power and reach of his thrusts until she felt he'd filled her whole body, that she'd become only a shell around him and their baby. Pleasure pounded through her, pain sharpening it beyond endurance until orgasm shredded her.

She clung to him in the throes, the world heaving, the violent pulse of his own release sending her over more and more edges, screaming…and saying nothing.

She'd say nothing, for as long as she could. He'd hesitated to tell her. Maybe if she kept silent long enough he never would….

Aliyah stared down at her loosening pants.

She'd lost too much weight. Kamal had made the tight comment again this morning. It had been three weeks since she'd tested for her pregnancy. She was most probably nine weeks pregnant now. She knew she was. She just knew she'd conceived that first night.

But it wasn't morning sickness making her lose weight. She

had something worse, manifesting in perpetual oppression. Soul sickness. And Kamal, since that day he'd returned from his un-explained trip to the States, had felt sick, too.

He still made love to her with the same ferocity, and even more tenderness, still gave her everything he'd been giving her, his time and attention and support and encouragement, but it felt as if he was suffering from a mysterious ailment, sliding down a slope of deepening depression.

He moaned in his sleep, his body rigid as if guarding against constant pain. When he was lost in thought, he had the look of someone who was contemplating some form of serious self-harm. When he thought her preoccupied, he watched her, not with his former lusting indulgence, but with a bleakness that wrung her heart dry. His spontaneity had been extinguished and he seemed to be weighing every word he said to her. It puzzled her so much that, along with her own fear of saying the wrong thing now that she felt anything would break the thread, she'd become stilted, too.

So she was losing weight. Her appetite for anything but Kamal had vanished, just as she felt the dream she'd been sharing with him had. Her appetite for food, for life. For breathing. She'd been forcing herself to eat at all for her baby. Kamal's baby. The baby she'd have to tell him about soon.

She kept putting it off. And the longer she did, the harder it became to even think of the moment when she told him the heir he needed might be on the way. Or what would come afterward.

Either three more months in hell until they found out if the baby was a boy or if they'd need to go through this again, through as many pregnancies as needed to have the male heir. Or if she'd gotten it right on the first try, seven more months until she gave birth to that heir and Kamal took him and divorced her. Either possibility was so destructive, her mind swerved around it to avoid being damaged.

But there was one thing she could, *had* to concentrate on. Her health. This she couldn't put off or avoid.

She poured herself a glass of water, took it to the dresser, reached deep into its drawer, produced a vial, opened it, shook out a tablet, put that to her lips, raised her eyes to the mirror…and the glass clattered from suddenly nerveless fingers to the dresser, almost tipping over, splashing its contents.

Her face, her eyes. It was like looking into her worst days. Only far worse this time.

Her eyes filled and she slumped to the dresser, her head in her hands. She had to get herself together. She now had another life depending on her. She had to sustain it, nurture it.

She wobbled up straight, groped for the water, popped the tablet in her mouth, forced it down with a sip…and almost coughed her lungs out when thunder erupted behind her.

"*B'haggej'Jaheem*…what in *hell* are you doing?"

Kamal had been in hell since he'd come back from Vegas.

After Aliyah's mind-blowing welcome home, he'd almost never let her out of his sight, trying to show her what she was to him, to give her all he had to give and be hers. But guilt and compounding realizations had been corroding him. He'd take her, take all her fire and magnanimity, then feel like the worst monster in creation, taking such ecstasy from the very woman he'd abused. The need for penance, for punishment, hollowed him, and he started to think those should be worse than a slow, agonizing death. The one thing worse would be losing her. The need mounted inside him, reaching unendurable levels, wanting to shout for her to exact her worst revenge, stop giving him what he needed to survive, to take herself away forever.

He needed to hurt himself, he needed for her to hurt him. But she wouldn't. Worse, she'd remained as incredible as ever, and his self-loathing had festered within him until he felt it had eaten him through, that nothing remained of him but a shell.

He'd come here today to confront her. To put an end to this.

He needed a sentence, and he needed her to execute it. Now.

When he'd entered their bedchamber and seen her, misery and agony contorting her face, he'd known. No sentence would ever suffice.

Then he'd seen her swallowing a pill as if it was her salvation, and all the ugliness and madness of the past had crashed down on him. Everything had exploded, the shrapnel shredding the tatters of his sanity and restraint.

He hurtled toward her, swooped down on her, took her by the shoulders, snatched her up as if he'd snatch her back from the edge of the abyss she was throwing herself into again. "What was this? What did you take? Spit it out!"

"Kamal…what…?" she gasped, tried to squirm free, felt so weak and flimsy. He went mad with fear.

He shook her. "I said spit it out. I'm not letting you do this to yourself again."

"S-stop…l-let me go…w-what are you talking about?"

"I'm talking about your 'prescription drugs' and you're never taking them again. I'll shackle you to my wrist for the rest of your life to stop you taking them again."

"W-what prescription drugs? That was a multivitamin tablet."

The lies she'd told him once merged with her words now, with the words he hadn't shouted in the past, what he whipped himself daily for having held back, giving up on her, letting her down, abandoning her and leaving her prey to pain and desperation.

It all exploded from him now, roars bursting his heart with guilt and dread and despair, deafening him. "*Liar.* I know, Aliyah, I *know.* Remember when I asked you if part of your rebellious behavior as a teenager had been drug experimentation and you so vehemently denied it? I only asked because I found your stash of prescription drugs back in that condo you never invited me to. And I'm damned a million times over if I let you, my wife, my queen, the queen of Judar, fall into that depravity again."

And if he'd thought he'd ever known agony, it was nothing compared to what razed him now as Aliyah seemed to disintegrate before his eyes under the brunt of his words.

Her eyes seemed to melt, becoming so red he feared they'd shed blood, her face shriveling, her body crumpling under his fingers.

He crushed her to him, as if he'd hide her within himself, ranting now, mindless with contrition. "*La, la ya habibati, la*...don't, *atawassal elaiki,* I beg you, don't...*samheeni arjooki*...forgive me, please, please...I didn't mean to upset you, I'm only out of my mind with worry...for you...don't feel bad, *arjooki,* don't feel bad about anything, ever, it will all be all right, just don't give in, and this time I swear I'll stand by you, give my very life for you not to succumb once more to addiction."

Her weeping only spiked, until he felt sobs rattling bones inside her flesh, until he feared she might start breaking up inside. But what congealed his blood was what he deciphered between the sobs, words that damned him to hell all over again.

"Oh, God...so th-this is why y-you were d-disgusted with m-me...as I always feared you would be i-if you found out..."

"No, *no,* I only wanted to help you, but you wouldn't tell me the truth, and I didn't know what to do, for a long time, then I decided to make you admit it, make you accept my help and—and..."

Words would no longer come. For whatever followed had to be explanations of why he not only hadn't helped her, but why he'd abandoned her instead after doing his best to finish her. He had no words to express his shame, no strength to wield his guilt, had to save all of him for her now, for fortifying and restoring her.

Then she was stirring from her limp surrender to his ministrations, too weak to push out of his containment, but making it clear it was her desire. He gritted his teeth, decided not to let her go. He'd let her go, let her down, too much already.

He bent and swept her up in his arms, took her to the seating area by the sea windows. He placed her with utmost care on the couch, came down on his knees before her, a supplicant seeking only the gift of his beloved's peace.

Still keeping her gaze averted, she finally whispered, "Stop looking at me like that. I won't start spacing out on you under the effect of my 'prescription drug' if that is what you're worried about. That *was* a multivitamin tablet."

He surged forward, his trembling hands on her wet face begging her to turn to him, see the truth written all over him. "I don't care about anything but helping you."

She looked at him now. He welcomed the pain as the bitterness and disdain in her bloodshot eyes lanced through him. "Like you wanted to help me back then? You sure did a great job. Like my parents before you. Between the three of you, you 'helped' me within an inch of my life. So thanks. I don't need your help, or anyone's. And by the way, those prescription drugs you found when you came searching my home when I wasn't there..."

"Aliyah, *ogssemlek*...I swear to you..."

She rasped on, sending his defenses backing up in his throat, "I hid them because they were my shame, my dirty little secret, but not like you thought. My parents put me on them when I was six to 'help' me with ADHD. It took me over ten more years to find out that they'd long realized my diagnosis was either wrong or that my reaction to the drug was worse than any disorder. But they'd trapped themselves, and me. It was either take the drug and be a zombie or cut it and be suicidal."

At his agonized grunt, his surge forward, she put up her hand. She wanted him to stay where he was, wanted to finish this.

"I understood then," she murmured. "Why I always felt I'd been watching the world from behind a barrier. I swore I'd never take the drug again, that I'd cure myself. I fought long and hard until they let me go. Then I spent the first months living on my own in hell, struggling not to go begging to reenter my prison. I was an addict, as you accused. Whatever withdrawal symptoms you heard about, I had them. I fought with all I had, but people had a great time calling me names, the princess who dared live away from her parents, the slut who called herself a model, who tried to fill her life with friends after she'd spent her life as a prisoner inside her own head. But I didn't care what people thought, was determined to see the hellish phase through. But it dragged on until I almost succumbed and accepted that drugs and their horrible side effects were better than being torn apart.

"Then, just before I met you, I felt I'd leveled out, hoped what remained were the high energy levels that had caused me to be diagnosed with ADHD in the first place. Then there was you a-and suddenly I wanted too much, there was too much to hope for, too much to lose. I went up in flames—of a different kind, sure, but I felt the old agitation sinking its teeth in me again. I needed something, a psychological crutch. So I bought the drug and hid it, just to feel safe. I swore I'd never take it, and I never did. But when you asked me about drug experimentation, I panicked. I was so ashamed, couldn't bear for you of all people—perfect, in-control you—to know I spent most of my life as an addict and the rest in withdrawal. I thought you'd be disgusted with me. So I said no. But that wasn't a lie. I never willingly took a drug.

"Then you left me, and in the devastation you left behind, I *needed* the blunting the drugs used to give me. The pain was so bad I almost succumbed. But I didn't. It was still two years later that the real me surfaced at last and I began to see the world through steady eyes, to focus, to achieve. I started painting, learned to ride and sword fight. And just as I thought I'd found my way, my world turned upside down again, and it will never right itself…ever again…"

Kamal felt it now. The agony that stretched into infinity without hope of amelioration, the kind that drove men to end their lives.

But he didn't matter. Only she did. He had to give her an explanation, not to extricate himself of blame, but to show her that the suffering he'd put her through had had a logic to it, however misguided, so she could rationalize it, accept it then one day maybe forget it, let it stop polluting her memories.

To do that, he had to put his own life's first scar into words for the first time.

"When I was twenty-two, my lifelong friend and cousin Hossam died of an overdose. But it wasn't his death that scarred me. It was what had happened in the years before he died. He'd become an addict at fifteen and his transformation—the monstrous warping of everything I loved about him—was a slow poison in my blood. His parents and I tried everything we could, from support and therapy to desperate measures. And he'd writhe and spew hatred and ugliness at us until he was spent. Then he'd level out, seem to be on his way to recovery, and we'd be afraid to breathe for fear of disturbing the delicate balance. Then even under our unwavering vigilance, he'd find something to feed the vice that had consumed him, replaced him, left only his shell behind, a vessel to feed itself. The lies, the madness, the confusion and dashed hopes he inflicted on us all in cycles, over and over again, left us all devastated. Then he was gone, and he left us with one more agony, one more guilt—our relief that it was all over."

Silence expanded after his last word. Neither of them seemed to be breathing, their hearts seemingly stilled.

Her whisper, when it finally came, seemed not to be a sound, but an aching touch in his mind. "That's why you left me. You thought I'd put you through the same hell."

"I did think it, but that wasn't why..." His tongue thickened inside his mouth, twisted, as if with paralysis. And he knew. This was the moment of truth. The full truth. With himself. With her. "No, you're right. I might not have faced myself with it, but I must have loved you too little that I searched for a reason so I wouldn't fight for you, to spare myself the agony of repeating the ordeal. When I did, I convicted you without a hearing, on every count. Then carried out the brutal sentence."

Her eyes were bewildered. "On *every* count? I was guilty of more than one in your eyes?"

He lowered his head to her knee, demolished, unable to raise it with the insupportable burden of remorse and shame. And from the position, at her feet, in the depths of contrition and supplication, he made the rest of his confession.

After he was done, there was no silence, only the cacophony of taxed heartbeats and breathing, his and hers.

When she finally spoke, her voice was betrayal, hurt made sound. "Shane…I never even suspected…I believed the things he told me, too, without hesitation…he'd been so…so lovely to me, like the brother I never had…and that he felt that way, that he did that…oh, God…I was going insane in front of his eyes after you left me, and I was groping for explanations, asked him, and he told me of your meeting, how he tried to assure you there was nothing going on between us, that you said you couldn't care less what was going on, because you couldn't care less for me. And everything you did validated his words. But it was all his doing. He lied to you, to me, manipulated the evidence, and both of us…"

He captured her trembling hands. "And he paid the price for what he did to you, turned his loathing on himself, is destroying his own life as he almost destroyed yours. But I'm the one to blame. It doesn't matter what he did. It was I who sinned against you, I who had your heart in my hands and the power to hurt you, and I who put all my might behind the blow I wished would shatter you."

She shook her head. "You had reason…too many reasons. On

top of thinking me an addict, you thought me a slut—God...now I remember you called me that night, and I said I was staying at Sara's. But you saw me come back. There was nothing else you could think..."

He caught her face. He had to stop her. "No, *ya habibati*, you're not exonerating me. None of that makes any of what I did in the least justifiable. I was a sadistic, self-preserving bastard who went to destructive lengths to maintain my pride, my peace of mind, maybe even my status. And I pounced on the chance to feel justified. I deserve anything and everything in punishment. Punish me, Aliyah. You *must* punish me. And after you've had your fill, cooled your rage, healed your heart and soothed the pride I demolished, then demand your compensation. Of my very life."

What she did was break down.

Out of his mind with agitation, he surged over to her, hauled her to him, his arms flailing around her. "*La tebki, ya rohi,* don't cry, I am not worth one of your precious tears." She shook her head again, her sobs losing momentum. He hurtled on. "Tell me, *ya hayati,* what can I do to make you whole again, to atone? *Atawassal elaiki, ya mashoogati,* I beg you, demand, anything, everything."

She kept trying to say something, every time hiccuping, choking and giving up. Then at last her tears slowed down, her sobs died and she lay back in his arms spent, her eyes closed.

Without opening her eyes, she suddenly whispered, "*Habibatak, rohak, hayatak, mashoogatak*—your love and soul and life and worshipped one. I was only *maleekatak* before."

"You are my queen, ruler of my life, and everything I called you and a thousand things beside. You're everything to me."

Her incredible eyes opened, clearing of the terrible tinge of relived agony, something like restoration casting the gleam of serenity on their beauty.

"Are you taking back your decree then?" He stared at her, at a loss, mostly with shock at the teasing note entering her voice. Her lips were even twitching. "That's the problem with making too many undocumented decrees. You end up lost with no referencing index."

He still didn't know what she was talking about. But it didn't matter. His answer was the same anyway. "I don't need one. Whatever decrees I made, unmake them. Make new ones, command me, and I'll obey."

The lips still glistening with tears tugged into a definite smile this time. "Whoa. The king of Judar at my command. Almost sounds like you're abdicating to me."

"I am, abdicating all that I am to you."

She pouted. "You're just saying that because you know I'll never use that carte blanche. At least, never abuse it."

He took her hands to his lips, covered them in adoration. "And I'm only too sorry you won't, that you're the woman who owns me mind and body and soul because you won't."

"You really want to be punished, don't you? Who knew you had a masochistic streak. But since you do, I always wanted to explore some stuff, mainly with you helpless and me driving you insane."

He went dizzy with the pressure of emotion. "That's not punishment, that's reward beyond measure. Don't do this, Aliyah. Don't forgive me. And *b'Ellahi,* don't forgive me that easily."

"Who says anything about it being easy? Loving for a lifetime is hard work, the hardest. This is what you're offering?"

"For *my* lifetime, yes. And beyond, if there is one."

Her eyes melted again, this time with such pure emotion, he had to close his own eyes. He opened them again when she teased, "Good thing then I'm also the woman the throne of Judar needs."

All starting relief drained, oppression rushing in its wake.

This was no teasing. No matter what he said, she'd always believe part of his reason for being with her rested on the fact that she was necessary to secure and stabilize the throne.

"Make love to me, Kamal."

His whole being quaked at the quiet request. So subdued for his fiery queen. He raised his wounded gaze to her face, found the same calm in her eyes. *"Mashoogati..."*

"Make love to me now I know that you love me, too."

He surged up, buried his face in her bosom. "How *do* you love me, still? When I deserve to lose you?"

She stabbed her fingers into his hair, dragged his face up to her with a gentle tug. "Goes to show you how blessed you are. Will you now show me just how blessed I am?"

Groaning his love to her over and over, he clasped her to his heart, swept her to their bed and worshipped her throughout the night. And if he'd thought she'd given him her all before, he now knew how much of herself she'd been withholding. The levels they soared to, the profundity of intimacy now that their hearts lay wide-open for each other to explore and own, left them both shaken.

Then he watched her as she fell into an exhausted sleep in his arms, her face both ravaged by their agonizing confrontation and replete with the tempestuous tenderness they'd just shared.

He carefully left her side, dressed in haste, dashed to his stateroom, raised the alarm.

He'd now do what he should have done from the start.

He would set them both free.

Aliyah woke up in a new world. Of absolute freedom. Freedom of the burden of the past, of the shackles of memory. Of gravity. Of her very mortality. She felt like a goddess.

How could she not feel like one when a god like Kamal loved her with all of his being?

And he'd *always* loved her. The emotions she'd felt and would always feel for him were so limitless because even when her mind hadn't known it, her heart had felt his reciprocating involvement.

It had gone so wrong, hurt so horribly, but she'd been as much to blame as either him or Shane. He of course wouldn't hear of anyone's faults but his. He lay claim to everything, took full responsibility. Just like he always did.

But now that she knew what had happened, it felt as if the past had been erased. And then this ecstasy would have felt like too much, if they hadn't paid for it with heartache first. Now she wouldn't feel guilty or worried about being so insanely happy. And now her pregnancy wouldn't mean the end, it would only be the glorious beginning.

She hadn't told him last night. Last night had been about them, about erasing the ugliness of the past, and laying down the foundations to a future she could barely begin to envision.

But now she'd tell him of the new life they'd made together, the baby she now knew was formed of immense love on both their sides. And she had to tell him now.

She flew through the palace to his stateroom, dismissed the guards at the door, ordered them to clear the vicinity. There was no telling what her revelation would lead to with her perpetually hungry sex god. They hadn't made love on his regal desk yet.

She opened the door to the antechamber, tiptoed until she saw him sitting at said desk, almost in profile, facing two wide-screen computer monitors. Farooq and Shehab were glaring out of each.

Kamal was talking. "...and when you hear what I've done, you'll have to admit that I'm a genius. To my face this time."

And God, what a face. She'd never seen Kamal looking like that, face alight with mischief, humor fully unleashed, no-holds-barred delight flaring tongues of flame from his eyes, scorching her with love and longing, filling her with uncontainable impatience, the need to barge in, hurtle to him, interrupt his video meeting with his brothers and just have him with her again, *have* him, lose herself in him again.

But he was so focused on his brothers, on what he was telling them. This, and something else she couldn't define, made her pull back, refrain from intruding.

Now she heard Farooq letting out a huge sigh. "I'd like to do many things to your face, Kamal. I've wanted to since the day you turned two. And it isn't our parents' 'not the face' indoctrination or you being my king now that's stopping me from dropping everything and giving in to the urge. I just know you'll drill your way into getting what you want. So I'll tell you what you want to hear without hearing what you want to say. You're a genius, *Zain?* And as I suspect now, a madman, too. You scared the hell out of us the way you summoned us, made us interrupt our tours. I thought someone was dying. What's gotten into you?"

"You should be asking what's gotten *out* of me, what's no longer dragging my spirit down, crushing any chance of happiness."

Shehab tutted. "If I didn't know how you abhor anything mind- or mood-altering, what a fanatic you are about your health, I'd say you're on a very powerful, not to mention unpredictable high."

Kamal guffawed. "I *am* high, the highest I've ever soared in my life, and now I'll never stop rising. Shehab, remember that maternal talk you gave me before my wedding? When you wished me as much happiness as you're wallowing in with your Farah? Well, move over, both of you, for neither of you any longer holds the title of happiest man alive."

Aliyah's heart somersaulted in her chest. She didn't care if it was a physical impossibility. It did. It was even doing backflips. Kamal. The love of her life. The father of her baby-to-be. As deliriously happy as she was, so happy he was bursting with the need to shout it out to the whole world, settling for his brothers, the only ones he could share with.

Shehab groaned. "You're also the most aggravating one. Talk already, *ya rejjal.* What is this all about?"

Kamal swung a full turn in his swiveling chair, like a boy

bursting with glee. "I just finished a ten-hour video-conference negotiation *war* with every head of every house of the Aal Shalaans and the Aal Masoods, and every other major tribe in the region. And *I did it*. My marriage to Aliyah is no longer a requirement for peace, neither is our child. I no longer *have* to stay married to her, no longer *have* to have a child with her."

Air congealed in Aliyah's lungs, beats in her heart.

He—he couldn't mean…couldn't…

She watched as he exploded to his feet, threw out his arms wide and shouted an ecstatic, "I'm *free*."

And her world came to an end.

[faded text from previous page, largely illegible]

Ten

Aliyah had never run that fast.

But there was no escaping the devastation of Kamal's words. The magnitude of his elation at eliminating his need for her and her baby. The realizations.

It all made sense. Far more sense than his loving her all along, all-out and unto eternity. He'd explained it to her. How he was a man in a class of his own, who abided by rules of his own, who wielded both power and burdens no one else could even imagine. She'd known he'd do whatever it took to fulfill his duties. What was catering to the needs and illusions of a love-starved moron compared to some of the monumental things he must be forced to do to safeguard his throne and kingdom?

He'd declared his love because he'd still needed her till that moment. He probably hadn't believed her, thought she was abusing drugs again and he'd had to stop her any way he could, couldn't have her disgrace her position or abuse the body that was supposed to bear him his heir. What better way was there to have her do whatever he wished than to dangle himself, all of him, in place of any temptation…?

Dragging my spirit down, crushing any chance of happiness. Happiest man alive. I no longer have to stay married to her, no longer have to have a child with her. I'm free.

The words detonated in her mind, over and over, the memory of the joy on his face razing her with misery.

All those nights, all those days, all those things he'd said and done, that last miraculous night, and all that time he'd hated having to play his part with a ferocious passion, had been struggling to get rid of her, doing anything to eliminate her importance, his need for her. And he'd succeeded. It was over.

Her sprint came to a jarring end against something solid. No tears poured from her eyes, no tremors tore her apart. She wasn't even panting. There was nothing. So too much damage *did* deaden.

She welcomed the numbness, walked again, walked until she got out of the palace. She'd keep on going until she was out of Judar.

She'd never return.

It took Kamal three more agonizing hours of tying up loose ends before he could fly back to Aliyah.

He hadn't wanted to share the news, as he'd been bursting to, before every last tiny provision was in place and everything had become binding and irreversible.

But the throne of Judar was now secure. And so were Zohayd and the whole region.

And it had nothing to do with their marriage.

He burst into their bedchamber, expecting her to be still sleeping off last night's roller coaster, or at least lazing about in their apartments, waiting for him to come back, to share another flight to their own realm.

His momentum died as he searched the extensive place for her, found her nowhere, the inexplicable oppression, the hollowness that had assailed him even as he'd tied up his pacts' loose ends intensifying.

Which was ridiculous. He had to banish those superstitious residues. He *wasn't* living in dread of when he had to pay for happiness of this magnitude by an even greater devastation.

It *had* been fourteen hours since he'd left her side. She must have woken up, showered, was probably down in her atelier, maybe finishing his painting. Maybe today she'd show it to him now that she had no more to hide from him.

He dashed down to her atelier. But with every quickening step, the premonition crystallized into certainty. He wouldn't find her there, either.

And he didn't.

He came to a stop before her covered painting, his distress, its import, inescapable now. He felt sick with dread, emptied, because his world *had* been emptied. Of her presence. He couldn't begin to think how or why, but his heart knew, had been telling him for hours now and he hadn't been able to listen.

He'd look for her everywhere and she wouldn't be there. Not in the palace. Not in Judar.

Too numb to register pain yet, he uncovered the painting. As if he'd find clues to the reason behind her decision to end it.

It was finished. It was unsigned. As if she didn't want to leave him an admission it had been her who'd painted it. As if she'd left him a message that before she'd left him for real, she'd left him in her heart.

By the time he landed in L.A. twenty hours later, Kamal felt he'd aged twenty years. Forty.

Aliyah had left without a word. Not to anyone. She'd simply ordered a jet and flown away from him.

The one thing that had stopped him from plunging into madness when she'd remained inaccessible had been that his Judarian embassy men had assured him she was safe at her old condo.

She was safe. He'd tried to cling to that knowledge, to tell himself that nothing else mattered, that until he saw her again, he wouldn't think beyond that.

Yet he could do nothing but think, dissect every second spent with her since he'd laid eyes on her under the magnifying insight provided by all that he now knew, had experienced with her, examining and analyzing each in hope of formulating an explanation for her sudden departure.

By the time he was standing on her doorstep, he'd long consumed his stamina, his sanity.

Then Aliyah opened the door.

His whole being rioted at her sight, his abused senses soaking in her every detail. The hair swept back into a tight ponytail, the slimness encased in her old style of clothes, faded jeans and nondescript T-shirt, the colorless face.

But she left him starving for acknowledgment, for hope of reconnection, didn't even look up, just turned away. He followed her with dread and confusion finishing the job they'd started since he'd found her gone, into the place that had seen some of his life's worst moments, where he only expected far worse to unfold now.

Before he could find his voice, his reason, she turned to face him. "Call your guards to come carry these away."

His eyes tore from her expressionless stare, to where she'd indicated. *These* were two of the chests of jewels he'd laid at her feet during their marriage ceremony, which he'd transferred to Judar's embassy for her use on their visits to the States.

"You have the rest in Judar, but I had these delivered to me so I could give them back to you myself, as per the rituals of *khol'e*."

Khol'e. The word skewered through him. The provision in

their culture's matrimonial laws, where a woman "rips out" a hated husband from her life and heart.

She stood straighter, her gaze fixed on his. "*Kama gabelt mahrak wa zawajak, arrod alaik marhrak wa akhla'ak.* As I accepted your *mahr* and you as my husband, I return it to you and cast you off. I'm no longer your wife. Now take these and get out."

His heart had burst time and again as she'd droned out the pro-nouncement. That still didn't finish him. Nothing ever would. He'd never have that mercy.

One thing was left now. Irony. It all made such perfect sense, a masterpiece of poetic justice.

"So this is your punishment." He heard the bass rasp, dimly realized it was issuing from him. "*Ya Ullah*...not even in my most violent self-flagellating binges as I devised nightmarish punishments to fit my crimes did I even imagine anything like this. I never thought you'd be so creative in your cruelty, so annihilating in your payback. I thought the worst you could do was deny me the sight of you, the breath I need to survive, leave me with remorse and memories to finish me slowly. But you had a far, far more agonizing idea. You gave me every-thing first—hope in your forgiveness, belief in your resur-rected love, led me on until I wrapped miles of hope and happiness around my own neck, then kicked the fool's stool from beneath me."

Something horrifying twisted on her face, in her eyes, like a bird flailing its last breaths. Her voice sounded even worse as she hissed, "Get out of here. I can't bear to look at you."

And the dam of shock shattered. "I lied...when I said I wanted to be punished by losing you. I was playing the martyr and I take it back. Don't punish me this way. Do anything else. Anything."

Her face seemed to melt before she swung away. And he was catching her back, his trembling fingers, his working lips sinking into her flesh, her reality, before she disappeared. "Then leave me but just let me dream that you might come back to me, that you won't leave me forever."

A violent tug took her away from him, left her plastered to the wall, breasts heaving with agitation, eyes spewing loathing.

And he begged. "I took all the blame before, I still do. But I must now say something in my own defense. If you think I walked away from you and lived in peace while you suffered, that's not true. I paid with a hefty chunk of my sanity and soul. Ask my brothers. The only thing fueling me was rage, at you, at what I thought you'd done. It ate at me, at my humanity. Everything was ashes in my mouth, dead to my senses. But though you must punish me, you once loved me…"

The hard look in her eyes slammed a monstrous suspicion into him. "*Ya Ullah*…you didn't? Could it have all been a game to you? An act, from day one? You made me believe in you so that disillusion in you left me a bitter, damaged man, then this time around you made me surrender totally, brought me to my knees only so you can kick me in the teeth and shatter me? So you can twist the knife until you eviscerate me…?"

"*Stop.*" Her scream was a close-range bullet smashing the spiral of insanity. "You had your way. You achieved your objectives. What more do you want? You're that sick a bastard you want to keep slamming me around until you see me in a heap? You almost succeeded in the past, but you're not succeeding now, do you hear me? You made me and my baby redundant. Good for you. But I'll live strong and healthy for this baby, and I'm never letting you near it, near either of us, ever again."

Everything stilled inside him. Around him. As if the world had stopped revolving, in empathy with his confusion, then in awe at the realization seeping through him.

She…she was…*pregnant?*

Then more sank in, her anguish, her words…

And he swept her into his arms, panting, quaking with torment and stupefaction and joy. "How do we manage to do this? How do two supposedly highly intelligent people like us, who shared and share everything, keep getting their wires crossed so horrifically? My only excuse is that I love you so insanely, anything that hints at losing you leaves me unable to access my logic and restraint."

She pummeled at him, and the feel of her blows landing on his back and head felt like the jolts he needed to restart his life, to keep his heart beating.

"Let me go," she shrieked. "Or I swear you'll rule Judar with one eye. I *heard* you, you bastard. Why are you here? Why are you keeping up this sadistic pretense? You didn't finalize your bargains yet? There are glitches you haven't foreseen in the way still? Or did you find you can't get rid of me and my baby without repercussions to your throne?"

He closed his eyes and took her bombardment, physical and verbal, an infinitesimal measure of her retribution, his atonement, wished she'd stop being so merciful and inflict some real damage. But her blows lost their power, her sobs dissipating their impact until she expended her strength, the impetus of her fury, and slumped in his embrace, quivering with exhaustion, her eyes flowing with futility.

His own distress flowed, mingled with hers over her soaked face, the gusts of his upheaval surpassing hers in force until she stirred, raised stunned eyes, only to squeeze them shut on a sharp gasp when one of his tears splashed in one.

When she next opened her eyes, he could almost believe she'd give him his wish, do him permanent injury.

"Tears?" she hissed. "It's that bad? You're going to be dethroned unless you get me back, or what? Of all the award-winning acts you churn up on demand, this one takes the cake. I didn't even think you came equipped with tear glands..."

He clamped his mouth over hers, swallowed her abuse,

only because he felt her heart racing beneath his, felt every word compounding her distress. She struggled in his arms again, bit into his lips, and he persisted, gentle, begging, letting her taste his tears and entreaty as he lapped up hers. Her struggle gradually dwindled, until she was sobbing, letting him worship her. When he felt he had a chance of being heard, he pulled away.

"Will my storm of a queen let me get a word in now? Yes, I've done the impossible to make everyone agree in binding pacts that our marriage is no longer needed, our child no longer a factor in the peace. In fact, I could have done that all along."

The hatred that had been ratcheting up in her eyes jerked at his last statement. *"What?"*

He smoothed an aching palm down her cooling-with-tears cheek, attempted a smile that came out a grimace. "I was always the one with enough power and in possession of all the vital keys to bring about this resolution. But I didn't even hint at it, not even to my brothers. In fact, not even to myself. Can't you guess why?"

Her eyes narrowed. "So you could force me to marry you under false pretenses?"

He couldn't resist. He took another taste of those lips that kept shooting him through the heart with more straightforwardness and bull's-eye insight. "Yes. So I'd have you without ever admitting my need to you, or to myself. Now I have terminated the need for our marriage, to Judar, to Zohayd and to all others. It was the only way I could prove to you that I'm yours forever only because I can't survive without you, that the only need for our child and as many children as you want or can give me is my need to fill my world with little Aliyahs."

The betrayal in her eyes turned to disbelief, then to such heartrending hesitation and vulnerability.

And he knew he had to take the biggest leap, risk the most in his life. He could be throwing away his very life. But he had to do it, had to set her free completely and pray she might one day heal enough, feel enough again to let him back into her heart.

He forced himself to take his arms off her, to step away.

Then he said, "I accept you *khol'e*, Aliyah."

Aliyah jerked at Kamal's solemn tone, his fervent look, felt slammed down again just as she'd started to rise.

She stared at him, lost, as he went on, "Even if you retract it, *I'll* throw the oath of divorce on you."

And furious pain exploded out of her. "Okay, now I'm sure you're a terminally warped, heartless…"

Her tirade choked off as he went down on one knee before her. "I'm heartless only because you are my heart, *ya galbi*, and I'm letting you go. Then once you are certain you are free of all obligations and duties and that I have no hidden agendas, I'll prostrate myself before you, no matter if it takes my lifetime, until you accept to remarry me, this time to save not the throne, but my life. If you think it worth saving, that is."

Tears surged from her depths like a geyser. "God, you maddening, heartbreaking man…s-stop. If one letter of what y-you just said isn't the whole truth, just stop now. If I'm not r-really as vital to you as you are to me, stop, don't promise more than what you feel. I just need the truth. I can't live with anything less from you anymore. I did before and it almost destroyed me. But I'm no longer free to risk my life and my well-being. I owe it to my baby to be whole."

The new lines that seemed to have been etched in his face since she'd last seen him deepened as he reached for her hands, took them to his lips, buried trembling kisses in them. "*Ya maleekhat hayati*, I'll prove to you this is not even the whole truth. I once said I'd pay any price to atone for my crimes, offer any proof that my life, the world, means nothing without you, without your trust and love. And I know now what it will take. I will give up all my affluence and I'll abdicate my throne."

She gasped at his steel-laced finality. "You know you can't do any of that!"

He rose slowly to his feet. "I can. The throne is secure now whether it is I who sits on it or not. As for my fortune, I'll give it all away. At any time, if you take me back, I'll just rebuild it from scratch. I did that the first time, anyway."

She shook her head, reeling. "E-even if all this is true…"

"There's nothing truer."

She held out her hands, begging him to stop. Her mind couldn't take any more. "Even so, I—I…you know I'd never let you give up anything at all for me, let alone all that."

"And that's exactly why I'm ecstatic to give it up all for you. I have nothing, nothing is worth having if I don't have you."

And she saw it all in her ruthless, blunt king's eyes. The calmness of conviction, the irretrievable intention, the soul-bearing sincerity. The mind-numbing fear.

He meant it, every word he'd said.

And she hurled herself at him, hugged him as if she'd haul him back from the edge of a chasm. "I believe you, *ya habibi*, I believe you, don't you dare give up anything, don't you dare."

On a huge gasp he crushed her back, rained kisses all over her, groaning broken words. "How will you believe me if I don't? How can I atone if I don't?"

"Oh, I believe you, I always did, here…" She pressed his shaking palm to her squeezing heart. "It was this belief that gnawed me hollow when it all went wrong. It wouldn't die even in the face of it all, and it's what kept me loving you. I felt what was in here…" She pressed his heart and he gasped again, buried his face in her neck, scorched her with the inconceivable treasure and unbearable pain of his tears. She hugged him harder, shaking, shaking him out of his surrender to guilt. She wasn't wasting one more second on what was dead and gone. She stuck her fingers in his hair, grabbed fistfuls, brought him up, groaning his enjoyment to face her. "And let's forget this atonement thing, too. I know you insist on monopolizing guilt but I already bought my shares of it. I never took you into my confidence, and I kept you at arm's length, confused you as I tried to pretend I was someone else. I gave you plenty of reason to suspect me, since I never let you know the real me, my real problems and fears."

He started to rumble that none of that constituted guilt, when she silenced him with a kiss. "But it has worked out for the best. It *has*. If you had stayed back then, I would have ended up clinging to you, drawing on your strength, and would have never found mine. It would have been unfair to you, and destructive eventually, to me and to our relationship. This way, I've been forced to find myself, become the woman I am today. You did go into great lengths about how impressed you are with her, yes?"

He seemed to grow darker, bigger. "You've just made sure there's no chance I will *ever* forgive myself."

He extricated himself from her arms, got out his cell phone and she knew what he'd do. If he'd gotten the convoluted mess between the Aal Shalaans and the Aal Masoods sorted out yesterday with a few phone calls, he could end his reign with one.

She pounced on him, snatched his phone and threw it away. "Get this straight, *ya maolai*. I'm Judar's queen and it's my duty to the kingdom and the region to keep the king who's holding everything together, the best king in history, on the throne, serviced and bursting with joy and satisfaction the better to serve his throne for the next sixty years."

His face seized. "Aliyah, *ya eshgi w'asbabi…*"

"You're my adoration and reasons, too, but beyond love, I'm beyond proud and privileged to be your woman, your consort. So you stay put on that throne, understand? Meanwhile, if you need to atone by loving me forever—and as it happens I'm free to love you back for the rest of my life and beyond—who am I to disagree?"

* * *

Kamal stood panting, filled to overflowing, paralyzed.

The miracle of her, of her love and forgiveness, the promise of a forever with all that. It overwhelmed him, taught him the meaning of humbleness, the ecstasy of it.

"*Enti kateer—kateer*…you're too much…too much…" and she was cleaved to him again, her tears mingling with his, the storm abated, finally free of doubt and insecurity and heartache. And he took her, gave himself to her, fully, no barriers, mental or emotional. And she took him, her passion a chain reaction with his, merging their flesh together in a dream sequence that seared him with its beauty even more after the nightmare of the end had been averted.

He came home, plunged inside her, drove in ferocious rhythms, shouting at the heights of the conflagration of dominance and surrender, weeping at the poignancy of union, of reunion, of souls and bodies sundered and now remade into one.

At the peak he drew away to watch her, his Aliyah, his queen and conscience, his mind and soul, his bliss and torment, taking her fill of him, at the mercy of the pleasure he inundated her with, magnanimous with her captivation of him, with her surrender.

Only when she started tumbling down the vortex of pleasure, crying out her love, convulsing around him, wrenching his release from his every cell, he joined her, spilled his seed, branded her as his once and forever, only sorry that he couldn't give her another child right now.

Then there was peace. For the first true time in his life.

Their union had started with their first eye melding, but this was the beginning of an inseparable life together.

He lay curved around her, his lips traveling her neck and shoulders, his hand luxuriating over the still-flat stomach where the living evidence of their love grew inside her, pride blazing through him, spilling on words of worship, pledges of forever.

Suddenly he jerked up in alarm, looking in stupefaction at the hand covering her belly. "Is this our baby moving?"

She dissolved onto her back and in laughter. "At nine weeks? Not even the super baby of super daddy would start making its presence felt this early. That's my appetite kicking in again."

He jumped up. "Stay right there, don't move or burn one more calorie. I'm fetching you a feast and I'm feeding you. I'm feeding you from now on. I'm no longer leaving you to your own devices."

Aliyah laughed again, threw her arms over her head in abandon, soaking up the sensual aches echoing everywhere inside her. "Aah, so we're back to overriding male mode. Lord-of-all-you-survey back calling the shots, all humility evaporated in a blast of superconcentrated regal testosterone, huh?"

He turned back to her, so beautiful and glorious and aroused it hurt. "Humility is still right here, growing stronger by the second. And it's yours, and yours alone, to exploit to your heart's content. But it's inapplicable here. When looking out for your best interests, I am unrepentant as well as unstoppable."

"And I bet even manipulative, too, if need be. All for a good cause, huh?"

"The best in existence." He smiled, that intimate, relaxed, devouring smile that made her go haywire. "You know me too well."

He ordered food then came to stand above her, his eyes blazing passion over her, igniting her yet again.

She moaned. "Well, I can tell you where food is concerned, you won't need to resort to any maneuvers. Now that you've let down your barriers, let me drown in your love, my appetite is in fine form. Let's just hope, not too fine a form." She held out her arms. "But now the only hunger I can't bear is hunger for you. How do you do that? How do you have me out of my mind, just by existing?"

He obeyed her and the pull of their bond, filled her arms

again, starting another of his potent seductions, murmured against her lips, "You send me to hell or to heaven with a word, a look. It's only fair that I do the same to you. But no more hell, *ya maleekat hayati*, ever. It's all heaven from now on." She arched up, tried to drag him to her, inside her. He still held back, groaned, "Before I take you again, will *you* take back your *khol'e*, take *me* back, already?"

And she did, took it all back, took him, all of him.

Forever.

Epilogue

Epilogue

Kamal stood looking over the Southern Gardens as the sun declined on the horizon. The festivities were as energetic and elaborate as ever even into their seventh and final day. Just like his and Aliyah's matrimonial festivities had lasted seven days after the ceremony and spanned the whole kingdom, so did those celebrating their firstborn's birth.

Ala'a Aal Masood. As they both intended him to be, the very embodiment of the elevation and greatness of the Aal Masoods.

Ala'a. His heir. The first fruit of his and Aliyah's binding, absolute and eternal love.

Aliyah. His eyes worshipped her as she sat across the terrace, holding their baby, her face ablaze with pride and tenderness and bliss. She felt his eyes on her, looked up, cocked her head at him, her waterfall of mahogany glory gleaming copper in the sunset. The look that flooded her face had him almost kneeling to kiss the ground in thanks. *Eshg. Walah. Ya Ullah,* so much limitless, unconditional love.

He soaked it all up until she had to turn her attention away to their fussing child, then he turned his eyes to Farooq and Shehab.

He found them both looking back on the women and children who formed the center of their universes, the core of their souls. Carmen was laughing out loud and waving to Farooq as she ran after the careening Mennah. Farah was cooing to her daughter Hayam, whom Shehab had named after the delirious love he said she was born of.

Farooq and Shehab looked back at him at the same time. A long moment of communion passed between them, before they sighed almost in unison and turned back to watching their families.

Farooq's exhalation broke the silence. "The irony gets to be too much sometimes. To be so indebted to Tareq. If not for that traitorous scum-of-the-earth cousin of ours, if not for his machinations and conspiracies, all this, all we have today wouldn't have come to pass. If each of us hadn't raced to counteract or undo his damage, we wouldn't have found our irreplaceable wives, wouldn't be deliriously happy today. Even Judar is stronger than ever."

Kamal exchanged a look of astonishment with Shehab, and they both laughed in stunned agreement.

Still laughing, Shehab caught the kiss Farah blew him, put it to his lips before taking it to his heart. "It's an incalculable debt indeed. Maybe we should pardon Tareq, let him back in the country?"

A second's silence was all that suggestion warranted before they all guffawed simultaneously.

"That would be the day. I can just see myself contacting that perverted disgrace." Kamal pretended he was reading a letter out loud. "Dear depraved cousin, now that the throne of Judar is secure for the next six hundred years, the family that disowned you in lieu of stoning you invites you to come back to plot Judar's downfall and the region's ruin."

Farooq, who had the most personal vendetta against Tareq, the man who'd smeared Carmen, named her as a mole he'd sent to seduce Farooq and set him up for scandal, rumbled in his chest. "I say we do invite him back, to a solitary cell where he belongs. I'd drag him back myself, preferably over broken glass."

Shehab nudged him in the shoulder. "Let it go, *ya akhi.* He's not worth your angst. And then his danger to the throne of Judar and to anyone else is over. The way we have him…*regulated*…in his exile isn't much better than solitary confinement."

Kamal watched his brothers debate before he decided it was time to bring up what he'd been thinking about. "Speaking of the throne, we tossed it to each other to save it, but now that it's saved, you should take it back, Farooq. You are firstborn, and your place is on it."

Farooq looked genuinely taken aback for a moment before he drawled, "I beg to differ here, Kamal. When it was time to choose, I chose Carmen. You're the one who deserves the throne."

Kamal shrugged. "I'm no different from either of you. I *did* choose Aliyah. I was going to give up the throne to prove to her that I wanted her and her alone. She was the one who stopped me, who believed me and in me without proof. But I would still do it, without hesitation, if it ever came to a choice."

Farooq shook his head. "You're still the one who did save it, and in a much better and permanent method than any of us dreamed possible. To think you could have done it all along but used the situation to get Aliyah back, kept everyone in the dark. Even yourself, I suspect."

"And this makes me a king under false pretenses."

Farooq shook his head again. "Whatever led to this point, and as much as it pains me to say it, you make the best king among us."

Kamal made a face at him. "Hurts, eh? To admit that about your 'baby' brother?"

Farooq smiled broadly. "Like hell." Then he sighed. "And then it's not only you who's the most fitting king. Your wife is also the fittest among our wives from birth for the role of queen."

Shehab came between his brothers, slapped them both on the back before putting an arm over Kamal's shoulders. "And Farooq and I are perfect for our roles. After all, who better than your older brothers to keep you in line?"

At that moment Aliyah turned around eagerly, beckoned to him. And Kamal laughed. "Her, that's who."

He extricated himself from Shehab's arm, streaked across the terrace and rushed into her arms to the sound of his brothers' mocking, if fully empathizing, laughter.

* * * * *

If you loved the THRONE OF JUDAR *stories,*
don't miss Olivia Gates's next passionate, provocative
miniseries, THE CASTALDINI CROWN,
starting in May 2009!
Only from Silhouette Desire.

Turn the page for a sneak preview of
AFTERSHOCK, *a new anthology*
featuring New York Times *bestselling author*
Sharon Sala.

Available October 2008.

n●cturne™

Dramatic and sensual tales of paranormal romance.

Her parents had been killed in a car wreck when she w
twenty-one. And except for a few friends—and most recently her

Chapter 1

October
New York City

Nicole Masters was sitting cross-legged on her sofa while a cold autumn rain peppered the windows of her fourth-floor apartment. She was poking at the ice cream in her bowl and trying not to be in a mood.

Six weeks ago, a simple trip to her neighborhood pharmacy had turned into a nightmare. She'd walked into the middle of a robbery. She never even saw the man who shot her in the head and left her for dead. She'd survived, but some of her senses had not. She was dealing with short-term memory loss and a tendency to stagger. Even though she'd been told the problems were most likely temporary, she waged a daily battle with depression.

Her parents had been killed in a car wreck when she was twenty-one. And except for a few friends—and most recently her boyfriend, Dominic Tucci, who lived in the apartment right above hers, she was alone. Her doctor kept reminding her that she should be grateful to be alive, and on one level she knew he was right. But he wasn't living in her shoes.

If she'd been anywhere else but at that pharmacy when the robbery happened, she wouldn't have died twice on the way to the hospital. Instead of being grateful that she'd survived, she couldn't stop thinking of what she'd lost.

But that wasn't the end of her troubles. On top of everything else, something strange was happening inside her head. She'd begun to hear odd things: sounds, not voices—at least, she didn't think it was voices. It was more like the distant noise of rapids—a rush of wind and water inside her head that, when it came, blocked out everything around her. It didn't happen often, but when it did, it was frightening, and it was driving her crazy.

The blank moments, which is what she called them, even had a rhythm. First there came that sound, then a cold sweat, then panic with no reason. Part of her feared it was the beginning of an emotional breakdown. And part of her feared it wasn't—that it was going to turn out to be a permanent souvenir of her resurrection.

Frustrated with herself and the situation as it stood, she upped the sound on the TV remote. But instead of *Wheel of Fortune,* an announcer broke in with a special bulletin.

"This just in. Police are on the scene of a kidnapping that occurred only hours ago at The Dakota. Molly Dane, the six-year-old daughter of one of Hollywood's blockbuster stars, Lyla Dane, was taken by force from the family apartment. At this time they have yet to receive a ransom demand. The housekeeper was seriously injured during the abduction, and is, at the present time, in surgery. Police are hoping to be able to talk to her once she regains consciousness. In the meantime, we are going now to a press conference with Lyla Dane."

Horrified, Nicole stilled as the cameras went live to where the actress was speaking before a bank of microphones. The shock and terror in Lyla Dane's voice were physically painful to watch. But even though Nicole kept upping the volume, the sound continued to fade.

Just when she was beginning to think something was wrong with her set, the broadcast suddenly switched from the Dane press conference to what appeared to be footage of the kidnapping, beginning with footage from inside the apartment.

When the front door suddenly flew back against the wall and four men rushed in, Nicole gasped. Horrified, she quickly realized that this must have been caught on a security camera inside the Dane apartment.

As Nicole continued to watch, a small Asian woman, who she guessed was the maid, rushed forward in an effort to keep them out. When one of the men hit her in the face with his gun, Nicole moaned. The violence was too reminiscent of what she'd lived through. Sick to her stomach, she fisted her hands against her belly, wishing it was over, but unable to tear her gaze away.

When the maid dropped to the carpet, the same man followed with a vicious kick to the little woman's midsection that lifted her off the floor.

"Oh, my God," Nicole said. When blood began to pool beneath the maid's head, she started to cry.

As the tape played on, the four men split up in different directions. The camera caught one running down a long marble hallway, then disappearing into a room. Moments later he reappeared, carrying a little girl, who Nicole assumed was Molly Dane. The child was wearing a pair of red pants and a white turtleneck sweater, and her hair was partially blocking her abductor's face as he carried her down the hall. She was kicking and screaming in his arms, and when he slapped her, it elicited an agonized scream that brought the other three running. Nicole watched in horror as one of them ran up and put his hand over Molly's face. Seconds later, she went limp.

One moment they were in the foyer, then they were gone.

Nicole jumped to her feet, then staggered drunkenly. The bowl of ice cream she'd absentmindedly placed in her lap shattered at her feet, splattering glass and melting ice cream everywhere.

The picture on the screen abruptly switched from the kidnapping to what Nicole assumed was a rerun of Lyla Dane's plea for her daughter's safe return, but she was numb.

Before she could think what to do next, the doorbell rang. Startled by the unexpected sound, she shakily swiped at the tears and took a step forward. She didn't feel the glass shards piercing her feet until she took the second step. At that point, sharp pains shot through her foot. She gasped, then looked down in confusion. Her legs looked as if she'd been running through mud, and she was standing in broken glass and ice cream, while a thin ribbon of blood seeped out from beneath her toes.

"Oh, no," Nicole mumbled, then stifled a second moan of pain.

The doorbell rang again. She shivered, then clutched her head in confusion.

"Just a minute!" she yelled, then tried to sidestep the rest of the debris as she hobbled to the door.

When she looked through the peephole in the door, she didn't know whether to be relieved or regretful.

It was Dominic, and as usual, she was a mess.

Nicole smiled a little self-consciously as she opened the door to let him in. "I just don't know what's happening to me. I think I'm losing my mind."

"Hey, don't talk about my woman like that."

Nicole rode the surge of delight his words brought. "So I'm still your woman?"

Dominic lowered his head.

Their lips met.

The kiss proceeded.

Slowly.

Thoroughly.

* * * * *

Be sure to look for the
AFTERSHOCK anthology next month,
as well as other exciting paranormal stories
from Silhouette Nocturne.
Available in October wherever books are sold.

nocturne™

NEW YORK TIMES BESTSELLING AUTHOR

SHARON SALA

JANIS REAMES HUDSON
DEBRA COWAN

———

AFTERSHOCK

Three women are brought to the brink of death...
only to discover the aftershock of their trauma has
left them with unexpected and unwelcome gifts of
paranormal powers. Now each woman must learn to
accept her newfound abilities while fighting for life,
love and second chances....

Available October wherever books are sold.

www.eHarlequin.com
www.paranormalromanceblog.wordpress.com   SN61796

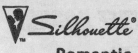

Romantic
SUSPENSE

**Sparked by Danger,
Fueled by Passion.**

USA TODAY bestselling author

Merline Lovelace

Undercover Wife

Secret agent Mike Callahan, code name Hawkeye,
objects when he's paired with sophisticated
Gillian Ridgeway on a dangerous spy mission
to Hong Kong. Gillian has secretly been in love
with him for years, but Hawk is an overprotective
man with a wounded past that threatens to
resurface. Now the two must put their lives—
and hearts—at risk for each other.

Available October wherever books are sold.

Visit Silhouette Books at www.eHarlequin.com   SRS27601

REQUEST YOUR FREE BOOKS!

2 FREE NOVELS
PLUS 2
FREE GIFTS!

Passionate, Powerful, Provocative!

YES! Please send me 2 FREE Silhouette Desire® novels and my 2 FREE gifts (gifts are worth about $10). After receiving them, if I don't wish to receive any more books, I can return the shipping statement marked "cancel". If I don't cancel, I will receive 6 brand-new novels every month and be billed just $4.05 per book in the U.S. or $4.74 per book in Canada, plus 25¢ shipping and handling per book and applicable taxes, if any*. That's a savings of almost 15% off the cover price! I understand that accepting the 2 free books and gifts places me under no obligation to buy anything. I can always return a shipment and cancel at any time. Even if I never buy another book, the two free books and gifts are mine to keep forever.   225 SDN ERVX   326 SDN ERVM

Name	(PLEASE PRINT)	
Address		Apt. #
City	State/Prov.	Zip/Postal Code

Signature (if under 18, a parent or guardian must sign)

Mail to the **Silhouette Reader Service:**
IN U.S.A.: P.O. Box 1867, Buffalo, NY 14240-1867
IN CANADA: P.O. Box 609, Fort Erie, Ontario L2A 5X3

Not valid to current subscribers of Silhouette Desire books.

Want to try two free books from another line?
Call 1-800-873-8635 or visit www.morefreebooks.com.

* Terms and prices subject to change without notice. N.Y. residents add applicable sales tax. Canadian residents will be charged applicable provincial taxes and GST. Offer not valid in Quebec. This offer is limited to one order per household. All orders subject to approval. Credit or debit balances in a customer's account(s) may be offset by any other outstanding balance owed by or to the customer. Please allow 4 to 6 weeks for delivery. Offer available while quantities last.

Your Privacy: Silhouette Books is committed to protecting your privacy. Our Privacy Policy is available online at www.eHarlequin.com or upon request from the Reader Service. From time to time we make our lists of customers available to reputable third parties who may have a product or service of interest to you. If you would prefer we not share your name and address, please check here. ☐

SDES08R

Silhouette®

SPECIAL EDITION™

Tanner Bravo and Crystal Cerise had it bad
for each other, though they couldn't be more
different. Tanner was the type to settle down;
free-spirited Crystal wouldn't hear of it.
Now that Crystal was pregnant, would
Tanner have his way after all?

Look for

HAVING
TANNER BRAVO'S
BABY

by *USA TODAY* bestselling author
CHRISTINE RIMMER

Available in October wherever books are sold.

Visit Silhouette Books at www.eHarlequin.com SSE24927

COMING NEXT MONTH

#1897 MARRIAGE, MANHATTAN STYLE—Barbara Dunlop
Park Avenue Scandals
Secrets, blackmail and infertility had their marriage on the rocks.
Will an unexpected opportunity at parenthood give them a second
chance?

#1898 THE MONEY MAN'S SEDUCTION—Leslie LaFoy
Gifts from a Billionaire
Suspicious of her true motives, he vows to keep her close—but as
close as in his bed?

#1899 DANTE'S CONTRACT MARRIAGE—Day Leclaire
The Dante Legacy
Forced to marry to protect an infamous diamond, they never
counted on being struck by The Dante Inferno. Suddenly their
convenient marriage is full of *in*convenient passion.

#1900 AN AFFAIR WITH THE PRINCESS—Michelle Celmer
Royal Seductions
He'd had an affair with the princess, once upon a time. But why
had he returned? Remembrance…or revenge?

#1901 MISTAKEN MISTRESS—Tessa Radley
The Saxon Brides
Could this woman he feels such a reckless passion for really be
his late brother's mistress? Or are there other secrets she's hiding?

#1902 BABY BENEFITS—Emily McKay
Billionaires and Babies
Her boss had a baby—and he needed her help. How could she
possibly deny him…how could she ever resist him?

SDCNM0908